MORE GREAT REA~~DS~~
AUTHOR/ILLUSTRATO~~R~~

The first book in *Theodore and the Enchanted Bookstore* series illustrated by J.H. Winter.

Labeled "unadoptable," by shelter staff, Theodore mires in gloom until a kind-eyed stranger with a pocket full of handcrafted jerky and a quirky smile, rescues Theodore and brings him to his curious Bookstore. Though overwhelmed at first, Theodore soon finds both his new friend and the odd bookstore are welcoming hosts, despite the Corgi's run of clumsy mishaps. And while Theodore's formerly dull and lonely life fades to memory, a new, adventurous one blooms before him—for hidden amongst the dusty stacks of books and things at the Enchanted Bookstore, waits a peculiar little man with a set of the most magical, Spectacular Spectacles imaginable.

Illustrator J.H. Winter adds author credit to book four and beyond of *Theodore and the Enchanted Bookstore* .

This time around, Theodore's off on an adventure of his own! It will be a tough one. He'll doubt he can do it. But there's a magical treasure to find for the bookstore. One hidden somewhere in Neverland. Without it, and other magical objects hiding in other stories, the future of *The Enchanted Bookstore* and the magical creatures housed within its walls, is a grim one. An unthinkable one. A future, Theodore must prevent!

AND ANOTHER GREAT SERIES FOR KIDS!

Mysterious Monsters is a humorous six-book early chapter book series full of mystery and adventure. When Marcus Mattigan, star of the popular show "Monstrous Lies with Marcus Mattigan" offers to let his kids, Maddie, Max, and Theo, travel around the country with him as he exposes frauds and fakes, the trio manages to find and capture the world's most mysterious and elusive creatures--and then to hide them in their increasingly crowded basement. As you can imagine, with each book, the situation gets more and more hairy.

Buy the series (pictured) or separately: *Bigfoot, Alien, Vampire, Ghost, Werewolf,* and *The Collector*

Corgi❤bits

An imprint of Incorgnito Publishing Press

WISHWEAVER

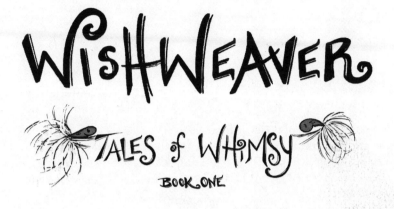

TALES of WHIMSY

BOOK ONE

J.H. WINTER

Wishweaver
Tales of Whimsy

For more information, to inquire about rights to this or other works, or to purchase copies for special educational, business, or sales promotional uses please write to:

Incorgnito Publishing Press LLC
1651 Devonshire Lane
Sarasota, FL 34236

FIRST EDITION

Printed in the United States of America

ISBN 978-1-944589-39-4

10 9 8 7 6 5 4 3 2 1

For
James and Lizzie,
My Wishes in the Wind.

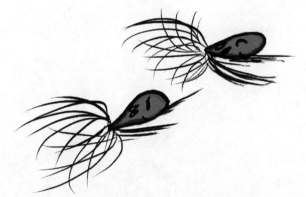

CROCHET YOUR VERY OWN WHIMSY AND FLIT!

Not only is J.H. Winter, an author and illustrator, she's also a whiz with a crochet hook!

Her whimsical designs are shared on her blog and YouTube channel: Ink & Stitches!

To get your free pattern to create your very own Whimsy, along with her best friend, Flit, head over to her blog.
http://blog.jhwinter.com

Don't know how to crochet? Not to worry! She's got you covered there too, on Ink & Stitches YouTube!

https://www.youtube.com/inkstitches

CONTENTS

CHAPTER ONE
WISHING

The West Wind had always been the connecting force between the Wishweaver of old and the one yet to take her place. It blew and it blew. Without excuse. Without explanation. It just was. It was life. A force to be reckoned with. And, above all, a conduit of magic. The magic to grant wishes.

For years, wishes had gone unheard. Unanswered. Perhaps a wisher was lucky and, by whatever force, stitched things together without sense, their wish was answered. But for most, wishing was like sending a hope into a deep cavern… only for it to be eaten away by a power which cared little for the wants of others.

There was a reason for that. There was always a reason.

One that those in Weyburn tried not to think about. For when the last Wishweaver had been among them, they had made a grave mistake. It was said around Weyburn that wishers had grown selfish with their wishing. So much so, they'd begun wishing for ridiculous wants because all of their needs had already been met.

"I want to glow blue!" one firefly had wished.

"A twirlier tail," said a pig.

"Hair would be nice," the crocodile who was never meant to have hair said. They were never satisfied.

It was said that the Wishweaver had grown exhausted to the point where her power had been used up. Gone. Lost to the cosmos. When she'd passed from this world to the next, another Wishweaver hadn't been born to take her place.

The home of the Wishweaver was in the hollow of an ancient oak tree, preserved just as she'd left it. It became a sacred place where many felt their wishes would be heard if they just took the journey to stand beneath the shade of its branches. Every Wishweaver had lived there and, perhaps one day, another would again.

Weyburn could only hope. Until then, they would wait.

The animals would con-
tinue the tradition of
planting milk-
weed

seeds so that more milkweed pods would grow. When the pods opened in the peak heat of summer to release their seed-lings—such adorable

little wisps—there
would be web enough
to catch them so the cycle
could continue. The orb spiders made sure of it.

For when a new Wishweaver came to take
her place in the ancient oak tree, they would
need wisps. Beautiful, delicate riders of the West
Wind; the only thing able to hold a Wishweaver's magic. That made their magic portable, to
be used by another. It
was a relationship, a

partnership
cultivated
through time,
which is indeed the
best kind to have.

******

When Whimsy looked up
at the skies above, she saw they
were covered in webs. Her siblings
were up there, mending old webs and
building new ones. They were very creative
in their construction of them. No two looked the
same.

"What'cha lookin' at, Whimsy?" asked the
small wisp cradled in her front legs.

"A place I never plan to go,"
Whimsy said.

"Where's that?"

"Up." The nerves roiled
in her stomach just from
thinking about how high

her siblings climbed. "I'm happy to stay firmly planted on the ground with you and the other wisps. Besides, someone has to take care of you."

"A spider who doesn't like high places. Not much sense in that," said the wisp as she also looked to the heavens. "I loved the feeling of the wind surrounding me, taking me wherever it wanted to go. It's so free up there. Sometimes, we all need to face our fears, Whimsy."

"That's what they all say. My family. The other wisps. But I'm happy right where I'm at, and that's with all eight feet on the ground. Besides, what are you afraid of?" Whimsy was always one to ask questions.

"What we're about to do."

"We don't have to. Maybe you can spend more time with the other wisps. I can choose another."

"No. No. It's my time. I can feel it. I will face my fear because there always must be an end in order for there to be a beginning," said the wisp.

Whimsy found a perfect spot not too far from

a mound where another wisp had been planted. She used two of her legs to dig down.

The wisp shook off her silky skirt and allowed Whimsy to place her into her bed of soil.

There, the seedling would grow to make another milkweed pod filled with new wisps for the coming year.

"Are you ready?" Whimsy asked.

"I am," said the wisp as she closed her eyes.

"I look forward to meeting your children soon," whispered Whimsy.

"Until then," said the wisp.

Whimsy brought the blanket of soil back over the seed and looked up again. Her family's webs would one day catch the next season of wisps.

Whimsy played her own part in making that happen. She was a Sower of Seeds.

She loved the wisps she met, and was the only one—who she knew of anyway—who took the time to talk with them. Whimsy walked over to get the next wisp for planting. On her way back, she heard a noise in the bushes.

"Ooh. Ooh. Ouch. Ouch!"

Whimsy followed the sound to its source. She

parted the fronds of a nearby fern and, hopping atop the wildflowers of a Queen Anne's lace, there was a dragonfly clutching one of its wings.

"Hello," Whimsy said, trying not to startle the poor dragonfly further.

"Ahhhh!" he said. "Don't come any closer! I'm warning you! I may be hurt, but I've a mind not to be eaten today, too!" The dragonfly held out one of its other healthy wings to illustrate his point.

Whimsy raised two of her legs and said, "I won't eat you. You can put your wing down now."

The dragonfly eyed her skeptically, then lowered his wing so that he could continue cradling the other.

"What happened…?" Whimsy waited for his name.

"Sidney."

"What happened, Sidney?"

"What didn't happen? That's the better question to ask!"

"Alright, what didn't happen, then?"

21

"I didn't fly straight! That's what didn't happen. I didn't pay attention, either. And I certainly didn't miss that big tree when it was right in front of my face! Believe you, me, I wish I had! What I did do was smack right into it! Stupid. Stupid. Stupid."

"Does this happen to you a lot?"

"More than I care to admit."

She couldn't help but laugh.

"Great, I see my suffering is funny to you, isn't it? You can add that to today's list of unfortunate events."

"I'm sorry. I can help if you'll let me?"

"Help me how?"

"There's one thing I'm good at using my webbing for."

"Building webs?" Sidney asked, momentarily forgetting the pain in his wing.

"Nope."

Whimsy walked up onto the flower next to Sidney, gently grabbing his wing, at which he squinted one eye—preparing for more pain that was sure to come. Whimsy spun her webbing like someone might spin wool into yarn. She used her legs to wrap her silk thread around Sidney's wing, straightening it out to help it heal. Finally, she tied her thread off and stepped back.

Sidney fluttered his wing. A smile spread across his face. He took to the sky, hovering above Whimsy. "Wow, you must be a Wishweaver or something!"

Whimsy laughed again. "I'm no Wishweaver, but I'm glad I could help."

"Thank you... I didn't even catch your name?"

"Oh, it's Whimsy."

"Thanks, Whimsy! See you later! I'm gonna go bug-hunting now. All this excitement's made me hungry again."

"Don't forget to look out for trees!"

The dragonfly turned back to look at her. "I won't!"

"Watch out!" Whimsy called, seeing

23

another tree up ahead.

"Whoops!" Sidney missed it by a hair. "Thanks again!"

Whimsy walked back down the flower. She thought about the actual Wishweaver and who the next one would be, or if there'd even be a next one. She wondered, not for the first time, why they continued on with the traditions of planting the milkweed wisps and building the webs to catch them if there was no Wishweaver who needed them.

"I hope I get to meet one someday," Whimsy told herself. "Maybe talking with them will help me answer all these questions I have."

She picked up her next wisp, who sat there smiling up at her with its silk arms raised. A tingling sensation spread out across her forehead for the briefest of moments. It was gone as quickly as it had arrived.

Whimsy shook the feeling away and walked her new wisp—a very talkative one, this time—to its new home deep inside the earth, to a place where the richest magic is born.

CHAPTER TWO

HIGH PLACES

"Whimsy! Come on! Don't be a sissy!" Edmund yelled while hanging from a high-up branch and looking at her upside down. It was the same conversation they had every day, and again, Whimsy stood her ground.

"I'm not a sissy! I've got work to do! There're wisps to be planted!" He didn't need to know she wasn't working that day, or the next for that matter.

"Oh, come on. Leave that to the other animals. You're a spider. What are you, scared or something?"

"Of course not! Do you want to switch jobs with me?" she asked, knowing what his answer would be.

"Not in the slightest! I love it up here!" Edmund said, swinging back and forth. He loved being in the trees as much as Whimsy loved staying on the ground. "See ya!" Edmund said before climbing back up his thread to continue weaving webs with the other spiders.

"Good morning, Lin," Whimsy said, passing by her friend who was in the middle of planting another wisp.

Lin Beaver patted down the soil with her flat tail, burying the seed. "Mornin', Whim! Where ya headed?"

"I've got a couple days off, so I thought I'd explore more of Weyburn. Wanna come?"

"Can't. Wish I could. My ma needs me home

right after work. They've been re-building the Redwood Dam over by the old Wishweaver tree. Said they need all the help they can get!"

"I may be heading out that way. I'll stop by if I do."

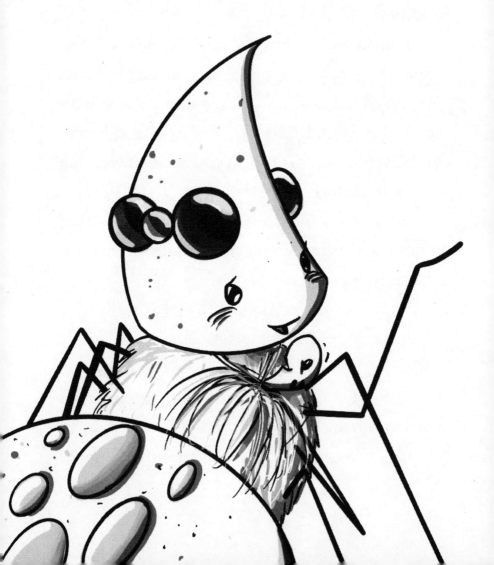

Whimsy left Lin to her planting. She made her way over to the group of wisps who were hanging around on webs, each waiting for their turn to be planted.

"Hiya, Whimsy!" came a familiar voice.

"Hey, Flit. Still there, I see," Whimsy said to one wisp in particular.

"Yeah, I haven't been picked for planting yet. It's okay. I'd rather hang around a bit longer anyway. Where're you going?"

"I was thinking of making my way over to the Wishweaver tree."

"Can I come, too?" Flit asked.

"I don't see why not. You'll have to hold on tight, though, so the wind doesn't catch you."

"I will."

Whimsy gently separated Flit from the webs and placed him on her back. "Ready?" she asked.

"Always!"

Whimsy and Flit set off through Weyburn to

see what adventures might be waiting for them through the trees.

******

Whimsy caught the sweet earthy scent of crawler biscuits cooking in a brown belly stove and knew Lady Porcupine was at it again. She made the best biscuits in Weyburn, as far as Whimsy was concerned, and it would be worth veering a little off course to get one… or three.

The willow tree Lady Porcupine lived in was as hollow as it was wide, the perfect spot for a porcupine to make her home. It was a cozy place to stay dry on a stormy night, and Whimsy had spent a fair few of those resting by the fireside, away from the whipping West Wind outside.

Whimsy knocked at Lady's front door and waited. She heard a rustling inside and pots and pans clanking together before the doorknob began to turn.

"Oh, hello, Whimsy dear. Flit. You smelled my biscuits, didn't you?"

"How could I not?" Whimsy asked with a smile. "I think the whole of Weyburn can smell those delicious biscuits whenever you make them. Lucky for me, I'm friends with the cook!"

Lady Porcupine laughed, shaking a few of her quills loose. Whimsy ducked to avoid them as they sailed past into a nearby tree. It was the one danger of having an elder porcupine for a friend. "Oops. Sorry, dear."

"There's one thing that's better than an apology," Whimsy said, looking bashful.

"How 'bout a biscuit?" Lady held out a plate with a pile of crawler biscuits on top still sending up dancing puffs of steam.

"One for each leg?" Whimsy asked.

She was met with a stern eye. "Why do you think the plate has eight?"

Lady Porcupine knew her well.

Whimsy came inside for biscuits and English Breakfast tea while Flit sipped a thimble of water that had been collected from a hole in Lady's roof.

"I wish that hole could be fixed before the rain starts up again. It nearly washed me out of here last winter when the worst of the rain hit."

"Where is it?" Whimsy asked.

Lady Porcupine pointed to the spot just above where Flit sat.

"Just there," she said. There was a bit of sunlight showing through. It wasn't a big hole by any means, but a hole was a hole, and where there's a hole, there's a leak.

Whimsy surveyed how high she'd need to climb to reach it, and since it wasn't too far from Lady's tallest shelf of books, she wasn't afraid. She climbed up from bookcase to bookcase, and once at the top, she was within easy reach of the problem.

From her spinner came silk. Whimsy took her sticky thread and wove it back and forth until the web was so thick, not a single drop of rainwater would be able to get through.

"You're all set!" said Whimsy, making her way back down.

"Thank you, dear. That's sure to keep me dry in the coming months, and you know what that means…"

"More biscuits?"

Lady Porcupine laughed and laughed. "Yes, dear. More biscuits."

"I can't wait! I'm going to eat them all!" Whimsy rubbed her belly.

"Speaking of which, why don't you pack the rest for your travels? You may need a biscuit or three where you're headed. Or perhaps you'll get hungry on the journey home."

"Thank you, Lady," Whimsy said, tying the

fabric-wrapped biscuits to her back.

She put Flit up on her shoulder again, and they left Lady Porcupine napping in her favorite quilt-draped rocking chair. Whimsy closed the front door behind her with a quiet click and they were off again, their bellies full, the sweet smell of biscuits fading away.

CHAPTER THREE

QUESTIONS

The oak tree they were looking for was a fair trek away. Edmund had told Whimsy a while back that he'd heard it bulged out in places and had flat mushrooms growing from its sides. The Wishweaver home was rumored to be at the very top.

Whimsy didn't expect she'd be climbing up to see it, but she'd love to see the tree nonetheless.

Perhaps it would give her some answers.

Whimsy had never ventured this far from home, and nor had she ever had the mind to, but things were changing. Perhaps she was changing. She was beginning to ask a lot more questions than usual. Why were they planting wisps and cultivating new milkweed plants? Why were they building webs to collect the wisps just to start the turn all over again?

"Don't get me wrong, Flit, I love what I do. I love spending time with you and the other wisps and planting them when they're ready. I could do without Edmund's teasing every morning, though. I could do without feeling like I'm not a spider or what a spider's supposed to be like just because I don't want to live in trees. But I'm tired of not knowing what happened. Why is the Wishweaver gone? And why hasn't another one taken her place?" Whimsy had so many questions no one seemed to know the answers to.

She needed to find the answers for herself.

"What if you don't like what you discover?" Flit asked.

"At least I'll know. I'll know what we're doing it all for."

******

They followed the river, knowing that, based on what Lin had said, they'd eventually come to the dam the beavers were re-building and that it would be very close to the old Wishweaver Oak.

There was a fallen tree up ahead that crossed over the river in an arc, landing on a giant boulder that stood its ground on the other side.

"Think we should cross?" Flit asked.

Whimsy looked at how high up it stood. Maybe it wasn't as high as the trees Edmund and the others were always spinning their webs in, but it still looked pretty high to Whimsy.

"Maybe we can go around it," Whimsy

said, weighing her options. She'd pick any other way across if there was one to be found. She knew she needed to face her fears like the old wisp had said, but perhaps she could put that off for another day.

"I'm pretty sure we have to get to the other side of the river at some point," Flit reminded her.

"True," Whimsy said.

"Help!"

The voice had come from the other side of the water.

"Yes, I'm here!" she shouted back.

"Where? I can't see you!"

"On the other side of the river! Can I help you with something!" There was a ball in the pit of her stomach. *Say no. Say no. Say no.*

"I'm stuck! Can you help me out?"

Whimsy took a steadying breath and looked back up. Now there was only one way across.

Up.

Whimsy squared her shoulders. "Hang on tight, Flit." Flit's wispy arms tightened and Whimsy climbed.

Her legs
shook.
Her stomach clenched.
But she continued to climb.

She got to the top of the log and never once looked down. Her nerve was a wishy-washy thing and she feared she might lose it completely.

"Okay there, Whimsy?" Flit asked.

"Under the circumstances," Whimsy said, her voice shaking. But they weren't across yet. She called out, "Where are you?"

"Over here!"

Whimsy went toward the voice, and it gave her the focus she needed to climb across the tree trunk. She still didn't look

42

down, but kept her eyes trained straight ahead. As she reached the topmost part of the tree, where it lay on the boulder, she had to look down.

Far below them, by the riverbank, was a pile of rocks. They looked to have just slid down the mountainside. Whimsy surveyed the rocks, but still couldn't see anyone.

"There!" Flit shouted, pointing to a spot among the rocks. Whimsy followed his gaze, and saw that there amongst all the rubble was a long, skinny green arm waving about, seemingly unattached to anything.

"Oh no!" Whimsy cried. She was too afraid to climb down face-first—or go upside-down for that matter. What she finally did was climb down backwards so that she didn't have to think about how high up she was. "Be my eyes, Flit. Please."

"Sure thing," Flit said, spinning around.

Down they climbed. Flit told her where to put her back legs, and although she wasn't steady, she was determined. Sometimes that and a little speck of bravery were all you needed in times like these.

Whimsy felt the rocks beneath her feet. She let out her breath. "There. Back on solid ground," she said, flipping around and looking for the green arm which appeared to be waving less franticly than it had been before. "We need to hurry."

They climbed up and over the rockslide to the animal trapped beneath. His voice had gone quiet and his hand rested gently on the rock beside it.

Whimsy went to work. She lifted rock after rock.

The more rocks she dug through, the more green she saw. Bit by heavy bit, Whimsy uncovered the creature. When the last rock was moved, she saw the poor tree frog who'd been trapped beneath them. His eyes were closed, and he wasn't moving.

Whimsy poked him.

Nothing.

"We're too late," she said, hanging

her head low. She picked up his limp body and held him to her, resting her head on his belly and trying to hear if he was breathing. She closed her eyes for a moment and felt that same tingling on her forehead. It came and it went just as before.

She felt a push against her head as the frog's chest rose and fell.

"Thanks," she heard before opening her eyes to see the frog who was now looking back at her, still held by her front legs. "You can put me down now."

"But you were…"

"Buried. I know. Terrible business. Just terrible. Minding my own, I was. Napping, too. Then my tree fell, and I with it! Top it off, the rocks slid down on me, they did. No time to get away! Glad you came by when you did."

The frog spoke so quickly, Whimsy had to focus to keep up with his words.

"Me, too," Whimsy said,

smiling at the silly little frog. "That doesn't sound like a nice way to wake up from a nap."

"No, miss. Can't say as it was. Anywho, thanks again. Gotta go! Think there was something I was supposed to do. Can't remember, but it'll come to me. Always does. Bye!"

The frog hopped away just about as fast as he spoke.

"Well, he got us to the other side of the river," said Whimsy.

"What an odd frog," said Flit.

"What an odd day," Whimsy said.

"You going to start climbing trees now, too?"

"Let's not go crazy. That was a one-time thing."

A dirt path appeared as they made their way beyond the rocks.

"Nice dry ground. Just how I like it," Whimsy said, scrunching the dirt with her legs beneath her, calmed by staying planted to the ground.

She reached a leg up to feel her forehead and found that it was warm. Something had happened, she was sure of it.

She hadn't heard the frog breathing. She was sure she'd been too late.

But then the same frog had hopped away.

CHAPTER FOUR
ANSWERS

The sky was a beautiful pink as the sun began tucking itself in to allow the moon its turn to shine. "It's getting late," Whimsy said. "Maybe we should find a nice place to settle in for the night."

"Good plan. I don't want to fall asleep and lose my grip or who knows where I'll end up!" Flit said.

Whimsy laughed. "There's no stopping a wisp

when the West Wind starts his blowing." She held up a leg and found that the air was still. "I think you'll be okay for now."

"Very funny."

They heard the sounds of breaking sticks ahead. Bushes rustled to and fro as thuds from heavy footfalls shook the Weyburn ground. The air smelled salty.

"What is that?" Flit whispered.

"No idea. Let's hide."

Into a nearby fern they climbed. Its fronds would hide them well.

The first thing Whimsy saw was a movement low to the ground. Then she saw the hair. It covered every inch of the creature—and there were a fair few of those, to be sure! But, no matter how long the thing was, its hair was longer. It shone a silver color that glowed in the light of the rising moon.

The beast tripped and fell into the gravel. "Blasted, confounded hair!"

The voice that came from the creature didn't seem to match the appearance of the animal that stood before Whimsy. Every time the animal tried to rise back up again, another part of their body dipped as their hair was pulled on the other side. From tip to tail, Whimsy noticed now, they were covered. Long flowing hair. As far as her eyes could see.

"Pardon me, ma'am," Whimsy said, stepping down from her hiding place.

"Who's there?" The hairy head whipped from side to side. "I can't see you!"

"Can you see anything?" Whimsy asked.

"Not anymore." The beast began to cry. Her cries turned to sobs as she gave up trying to get up. She was rightfully stuck.

"My name is Whimsy, ma'am. Would you mind holding still for a moment?"

"Can't seem to go anywhere anyway," came the voice through a shaky breath.

Whimsy worked fast. She might not be good at building webs like the other spiders, but she was the best at using her webs to mend and tie, and for any other un-spiderlike purpose.

Within a matter of moments, she had managed to use her many legs to pull back and tie each piece of hair into a ponytail, working from the creature's tail to its head. Each ponytail was tied

with web and then spun into a tight
bun.

As Whimsy pulled back the hair
around   the creature's face

to see what she was dealing with, she noticed teeth.

Lots and lots of teeth. Sharp fangs. Her heart stopped for only a moment before she continued what she had a mind to finish—to help this poor creature out, jagged teeth and all.

She tied a bun to either side of the animal's face and knew, for the first time, what she was dealing with... although the visual didn't make much sense.

"Hello, sweet spider. I thank you from the bottom of my crocodile belly."

"But I didn't think crocodiles had hair!" Whimsy said, all confusion.

"No, they don't. And they really shouldn't."

"Then why do you?" Flit chimed in.

"A good question, indeed. One I've been asking myself for years, ever since I made the wish to grow it in the first place."

"The wish?" Whimsy asked.

"Indeed. It was the last thing I wished for when the Wishweaver was around.

Or the last thing anyone wished for, for that matter. I'm pretty sure I broke the magic inside her by asking for something so ridiculous."

"Is that what really happened? That's why the Wishweaver stopped weaving wishes?" Perhaps she was going to get her questions answered after all.

"Well, no one can really say, can they? All any of us know is, that was the day she walked back into her house and none of us saw her again. We went looking, mind you, but we couldn't find her anywhere. Figure she died. She was getting up there in age. Not that I should talk. Anyway, that was years ago, and I can tell you this, my hair hasn't stopped growing since. The only one I have to blame is myself."

"I suppose that's true," Whimsy had to agree. A crocodile wanting hair did seem like a pretty silly wish as far as she was concerned.

"Sure, it is. At least I fared better than Lenny."

"Who's Lenny?" Flit asked.

"Lenny Firefly. He just had to glow blue. Said it was his favorite color. Never thought about the consequences of glowing blue."

"What happened to him?" Whimsy asked.

"Eaten. Stood out too much for his own good, I suspect."

"Eew," Whimsy said.

"What, don't you eat bugs?" the crocodile asked.

"Yeah, but not fireflies. I love watching them light up at night."

"You and me both, kid. I think of Lenny every night for that very same reason. Anyway, where are you two headed?"

"We were just on our way to the Wishweaver tree. I've never seen it before."

"Well, you're headed the right way, then. I

stay away from that place myself. Just go past the grove of bellflowers, beyond the ivy-covered cottage, and into the heart of Weyburn. You'll know her tree when you see it. There's nothing like it."

"Thank you, ma'am," Whimsy said.

"Call me Cricket, just in case we ever cross paths again." Cricket walked to the river without stumbling.

Whimsy glanced over to see the last silver hair bun disappear beneath the rippling surface.

"That was… interesting," Flit said.

"And enlightening," said Whimsy. "Now we know what the very last wish was that the

Wishweaver granted. We also learned something else…"

"What's that?"

"We learned that no one ever saw the Wish-weaver again."

"Right, that's because she died."

"Did she?"

"Cricket said she was old, and that was years ago," Flit reminded her. "Even if she wasn't dead then, she will be by now."

CHAPTER FIVE

BELLFLOWER GROVE

"Flit, look!"

The wisp raised heavy eyelids. They widened as they saw what Whimsy had just seen.

To say Bellflower Grove was just a grove of bellflowers wasn't giving it credit. It was so much more than that.

In the final light of the fleeting sun, Whimsy and Flit looked up at a beautiful clearing filled to the brim with bellflowers. The color of the sky matched the color of the flowers below. It was like the reflection of clouds in a lake, making the entire world look violet and pink, with sprinklings of white.

"Whoa," was all Flit could manage.

The only thing that separated the color of the skies above and the color of the flowers below was the rim of trees that surrounded the grove, lit now by firefly light.

The sounds of the fireflies filled the grove as they squealed with glee, zipping this way and that, dancing on the air currents and enjoying themselves in the rising moonlight.

"Hi!" one firefly said, waving his front leg for added enthusiasm. "Welcome to Bellflower Grove!"

"Thank you! I'm Whimsy, and this is my friend, Flit."

"Hey," Flit said.

"Name's Peter. You a wisp? Never met a wisp

before." The firefly flew up to Flit and surveyed him from every angle. "Love your skirt! Wish I had one, too. It's so pretty."

"Um, thanks?"

"Wanna come hang out with everyone for a bit? We were just about to start the music."

"Music?"

"Oh, aye. We fireflies love music! Did you know you can drum on the bellflowers?"

"No, we didn't," Whimsy said.

"Come. Come. I'll show you!" Peter rushed Whimsy and Flit deeper into the thick of the bellflowers. They weaved in between them and their sweet scent.

"Ready, fireflies?" called one of the other lights glowing from above.

"Ready!" yelled the rest, including Peter beside them.

"Hit it!"

The lights dove down, and Whimsy ducked out of their way.

As soon as the fireflies collided with the bell-flowers, the music began. Their chimes were loud, but uplifting all the same.

Whimsy and Flit watched to see how the fireflies made such wondrous music.

They looked at each other and burst into laughter.

· "Apparently, there're more things they can use their backsides for than just glowing," Whimsy whispered to her friend, watching the fireflies bouncing on their butts to make the flowers chime.

"That's talent," Flit said through a snort of laughter.

Whimsy danced with Flit. She couldn't help herself. She loved music, too, and Bellflower Grove seemed to be the place to enjoy it. They caught sight of Peter here and there as he bounced from one bell to the other. He waved down at them.

There seemed to be no end to the music. Whimsy didn't want to be rude, but she was growing more tired by the second.

When Peter made his way back around, she caught his eye.

He stood bouncing to and fro on the same two bellflowers while he listened.

Ding. Dong. Ding. Dong.

"We were hoping to find somewhere to stay tonight!" Whimsy shouted up to him.

Dong. Ding. Dong.

"What'd you say?"

Ding. Dong. Ding. Dong. Ding.

"I said, do you know of a safe place to rest?" Whimsy shouted a little louder this time. She looked up to see that Flit had already fallen asleep on her shoulder. She gently pulled him down to cradle him in front of her. He didn't stir.

"Ain't no place safer than Bellflower Grove. Come with me." Peter waved for her to follow behind him. He bounced his way past the other fireflies still making their music, but slowed his pace so Whimsy could keep up.

They made their way through the rest of the bellflowers. All the while, Whimsy took in the heady scents of spring.

Peter hopped off the last bell with a *ding* and flew just ahead of them. "I sleep just beyond the grove," he said.

And that night, so would Whimsy, with Flit held safely beside her.

CHAPTER SIX
THE HOLLOW LOG

"Wake up, Whimsy. You're squishing me..."

Whimsy loosened her grip on Flit, not having realized her dreams of losing him had tightened her hold throughout the night. They'd slept to the soothing sounds of crickets chirping their violin song, frogs croaking to the crickets' music, and the gentle breeze whispering through the tall grasses

Whimsy and Flit rested between.

Peter had come to sleep beside them some time during the night.

Whimsy pulled out a crawler biscuit from her pack and laid it down beside Peter while he slept, as a silent 'thank you' for his kindness. He turned over in his sleep, but didn't wake up.

"Let's go find our next landmark—an ivy-covered cottage somewhere deep in the woods of Weyburn," Whimsy said.

"Lead the way," yawned Flit.

******

Whimsy felt the hairs around her body flutter as the West Wind made his presence known. They always had a respect for his power, knowing that in order to continue in the wishweaving traditions, they wouldn't want to do anything to anger him.

She breathed in the new scents of wild lavender and pine. "Which way should we go?" Whimsy asked.

Flit looked around.

"Definitely not that way!" He pointed off to the right, where the ground looked shifty and unsettled. The trees were overgrown, creating the appearance of a dark cave that a dragon might once have slumbered in.

"Good call. Let's see... the river's still that way." Whimsy pointed to the left, to where the sounds of rushing water could be heard as it flowed downstream. "That means our only other option is straight ahead."

"There's your answer then." Flit tightened his grip on Whimsy. But the West Wind had plans of his own. He blew against

Whimsy, pushing her another way, toward the right, where the dark, ominous path lay.

"Whimsy!" Flit yelled, but she was too late to grab hold of him.

Wisps are good at one thing, and that is riding the wind—whether they want to or not. Against Flit's will, the West Wind took him. Up into the air, he flew, trying to grab hold of Whimsy's outstretched legs, but they had realized what was happening too late.

"Flit!" Whimsy cried, scrambling after him. He was moving faster than she could run.

The wind no longer pushed against her. It was Flit that he'd wanted. "I'll find you!" she called, hoping he would hear her cries.

******

Whimsy hurried. She couldn't let Flit get too far ahead, but she had no idea where the wind had taken him.

"Why are you
so mischievous?" Whimsy
yelled at the West Wind.

He didn't answer.

"Be brave, Whimsy," she said to
herself, pushing onward. "Flit!" she
cried, but there was no answer.

Each rock she climbed over
would bring her closer to her
friend. "Flit! Flit!"

She had to believe she would find
him.

Whimsy made her way over fallen branches,
through the thick spattering of plant life that grew
wild through the Weyburn woods, and past many
webs with spiders happily waiting for their next
meal to arrive.

Whimsy couldn't help her nerves tingling
about inside her stomach. It felt like the spiders
were watching her. She tried to avoid their eyes,

keeping her head down, but she could tell they watched her every move.

"Flit," she said, her voice quieter this time so that she wouldn't draw any more attention to herself.

The wind was picking up again, and his presence angered her. Why had he taken Flit? It made no sense.

Whimsy went to climb through a hollow log that looked like the quickest way out. In the entryway to the log, she hesitated, taking one final look back at where she'd come from. The spiders still watched her, whispering to each other words that Whimsy couldn't make out.

"I've got to get out of here," she muttered under her breath.

"I couldn't agree more," came a deep, syrupy voice from above.

Whimsy ran.

She made her way through the log toward the bright end-of-spring light that illuminated the road ahead. As the circle of light grew bigger and bigger, she suddenly found it gone. Snuffed out. She was swallowed by darkness and a still quiet, but for the sounds of scratching against wood.

Something was coming.

Whimsy looked back at the other end of the log and found that it, too, had gone dark. Before the light completely left, Whimsy saw legs reaching inside the opening from above and the body of the enormous spider they belonged to.

Whimsy screamed.

"Don't eat me! I'm one of you!" Whimsy couldn't believe what she'd just said. She'd never felt like one of the spiders, but the thought of being eaten by one really put things in perspective.

"One of us, are you?" came the same deep voice from before. "Are you really? You never even said 'Hi' on your way through our hollow. Right, Sid?"

"Right, Bax. Right, Bax. Never said 'Hi' or nothin'!" came a voice from behind Whimsy.

"Way I figure, you can't be somethin' you're afraid of."

Whimsy felt a bristly leg touch her chin, and it took everything inside of her not to scream or give in to their taunts.

"Who said I'm afraid of spiders? I'm just as much a spider as the rest of you." Whimsy stood her ground. She had to figure out a way to get out of there.

"Prove it," Bax said.

"What do I have to do?" she asked.

"I'm glad you asked. Follow me."

As quickly as the light had left, it shone back through the gloom. The body of a giant fur-covered spider came into view ahead as Bax

motioned for her to follow him. She felt a nudge
from behind just as Sid joined them.

"Go on. Get a move on," Sid said. "Bax doesn't
like waiting."

Whimsy walked back into the warm sunlight.
She looked around. Her conversation with Bax and
Sid had given the other spiders enough time to leave
their webs and surround her on the ground. The
cheers from the crowd and chants of Bax's name
left Whimsy with a sour taste in her mouth.

What are they going to have me do? she wondered.

"Quiet down. Quiet down," Bax said, only gain-
ing more cheers from the crowd. "Quiet!"

Silence fell through the hollow. Not a leaf moved.

Even the West Wind went quiet.

Whimsy could hear a muffled voice from the crowd, and looked around to see who it was.

To the left, a striped spider stood with its leg covering the mouth of…

"Flit!" she stepped forward to run to him.

"Hold it!" Bax said. "Don't even think about moving."

Whimsy and Flit looked at each other with fear in their eyes before she saw Flit glance back over to Bax.

Whimsy followed his gaze. Bax's eyes were trained on her. She noticed that one of them was missing and a scar crossed over where it had once been. He was scruffier than the rest of the spiders, and had only seven legs to choose from, as well.

"What's your name, kid?" Bax asked.

"Wh-Wh-Whimsy," she managed.

"Whimsy, huh? And this little thing you seem to know so much about?" He went over to Flit, who looked back at Whimsy.

Whimsy sent Bax a fierce look of warning. "Don't touch him."

"Oowie!" Bax backed up with a couple of legs in the air. "No matter. Now, I've a question for you Miss Whimsy, Spider Princess. If you are indeed a spider, as you say, then why're you traipsing around on the ground and not climbing among the trees?"

That was the ultimate question, wasn't it?

It was the one Edmund asked her on a daily basis. It made sense they'd all wonder that.

Spiders generally stayed safe by taking to high-up places.

Spiders, but not Whimsy.

"No reason. Flit and I were looking for something when he was scooped up by the

West Wind and brought here. I thought I might have an easier time finding him if I stuck to the ground. That's all."

"That's all, is it? Now that you've found him, what's next?" Bax asked.

Sid walked out from behind Whimsy to stand by Bax. She had nowhere to run. He smiled up at his master and Whimsy saw that he, too, was scraggly looking, with a fang missing and scars criss-crossing the top of his backside like the patterns of a weathered quilt. Whimsy brought her attention back to Bax.

"We were looking for an ivy-covered cottage," Whimsy said, standing her ground. She couldn't let them see how nervous she was or her shaking legs.

"An ivy-covered cottage, you say?"

Bax bumped Sid with his elbow and they both started laughing. The rest of the spiders thought it okay to join in.

"What's so funny?" Whimsy asked. "Do you know where I can find it?"

Keep them on something else. Maybe they'll forget about me having to prove I'm a spider.

"Oh, I know where you can find it, alright, and I'll do you one better. I'll even take you to it. Well… close to it, that is."

Whimsy didn't understand what was so funny about an ivy-covered cottage, but thought better of asking.

"That would be great. Thank you. Now, can I have my friend back, please?"

"Patience, princess. Follow me."

Whimsy sent a look of concern back to Flit, but then followed Bax, not knowing where the spiders were taking her.

CHAPTER SEVEN
AT THE BOTTOM

The cluster of spiders herded Whimsy toward an unknown location that lay ahead. She wasn't sure if she was still on the right path to the Wishweaver tree or if she was being taken off course. Whimsy only hoped that she could get them out of this mess, and so she kept her mind open to ideas that might be floating by.

"Nearly there," Bax said, glancing over his shoulder at her.

The air tasted salty again as they neared the river. The sound of rushing water began to grow louder. The further they went, the louder it grew.

Her ears became cloudy with the roar of it.

She watched the river flow in the direction they were headed. It drove on just as they drove on. As they came over a rise in the ground, the reason why became clear.

"We're here!" Bax shouted above the noise.

Whimsy looked around, but all she could see were trees. There was no cottage anywhere.

"Where is it?" Whimsy asked.

"Down. At the bottom," Bax said. He moved behind Whimsy to usher her forward. She pushed back against him, noticing what seemed to be a stop to the river.

But rivers don't stop…

And she was right. They didn't. They did, however, on occasion, drop.

Bax had Whimsy at the edge of the rocks, and now she saw why he'd been so helpful before, excited to bring her right where she needed to go. She'd known it had been too good to be true.

Whimsy peered out over the edge long enough to realize two things.

One: there was indeed an ivy-covered cottage at the bottom of the waterfall to the right. Two: she wasn't going to be taking the safe way down to get there.

Before she could take a breath, she was falling.

CHAPTER EIGHT
FLYING

Whimsy fell.

She couldn't scream. Her voice had left her.

"Whimsy!" came a familiar voice.

She arced her front half so she could look back up and saw that Flit was falling with her, the small downward wind from the waterfall pushing him toward her.

"Flit!"

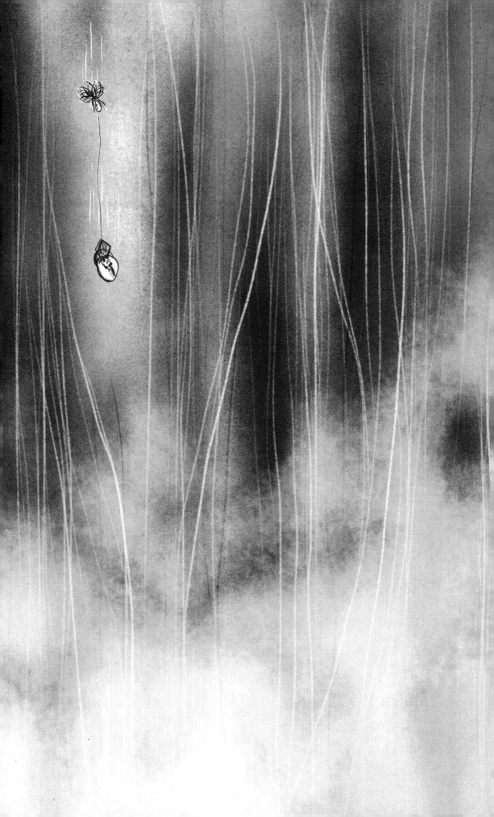

Whimsy got to work. First, she needed to get Flit. Then, somehow, she had to find a way of getting them to safety before they hit the water.

So, she spun.

As fast as she could manage while falling, Whimsy released a single thread. She let it grow longer and longer, trailing out above her.

"Grab hold!" she cried.

The thread whipped in front of Flit and he had one chance to grab it.

The two connected, and Flit was secured.

"Got it!" he yelled back.

They'd already fallen halfway down the waterfall by this point. Time for her next plan: getting them to safety.

What she'd been taught by the other spiders back home was the secret to spinning webs.

You couldn't spin a web without a breeze to carry your thread.

With two legs, she broke off the thread that held Flit and began to reel him in. She released a new thread from her spinneret until it became a long line trailing uselessly behind her.

They continued to fall.

She managed to cry out two words. The only two she could think of, in the hopes that he would hear her…

"West Wind!" she called. It seemed odd that he was the one who'd gotten them into this mess and also the only one who could get them back out of it. He was her only hope, but, as she very well knew, he didn't usually do as he was told. He was too wild to be tamed. But perhaps he would take pity on her this once.

As the pool of water came into focus, Whimsy brought Flit securely to her chest. "At least we have each other at the end," she said.

"No one else I'd rather be in this mess with than you, Whim."

She closed her eyes and accepted their fate.

I should have stayed home. I wish the West Wind would listen, for once.

A tingling sensation spread across her forehead. Whimsy waited for impact, but it never came.

Instead, she began to sail east as a force pushed her from the west.

She opened her eyes to see that her thread was now tethered to a nearby tree, holding fast.

"Weeeeeeeee..." Flit sang as he flew.

Whimsy laughed. The wind held her, helping her reach the safety of the tree ahead. She brought six legs to grab onto the bark when she came upon it.

"That was fun!" Flit said, and then he thought better of what he'd said. "Well, that last part anyway."

"You're crazy," Whimsy replied, although she had to admit that, when the West Wind had answered her call and she'd been flying instead of falling, it had been fun. "Perhaps being in high places isn't such a bad thing."

"Told you," Flit said.

"I remember."

Whimsy looked into the wind and said her silent thanks, then climbed back down the redwood tree. This time, she didn't back her way down. She approached the ground head-on, knowing that she wasn't going to fall.

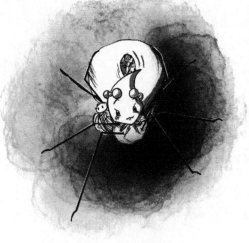

CHAPTER NINE

COTTAGE BY THE WATER'S EDGE

"It's not as big as I thought it would be," Whimsy said, surveying the little cottage with its thatched roof and small, red-painted door.

"Cricket was right about the ivy," Flit said.

Every inch was covered by the fast-growing plant with few breaks taken here and there to

allow a window to shine through. Otherwise, the cottage seemed green just like the rest of the nearby vegetation. Without the red door, it might have blended in completely.

"Who do you think lives here?" Whimsy asked.

"Beats me. Maybe no one."

"Don't you smell the smoke from the chimney?" Whimsy asked next.

"We wisps aren't ones for smelling," Flit reminded her.

"Of course. I forgot. Well, you can see the little puffs of smoke now and again, too. Look, over there."

Flit's attention was drawn toward the roof, where they both watched another puff of chimney smoke billow from the stack.

They heard singing by the water's edge and looked over to see movement on the other side of the pool.

Whimsy saw horns first. Great, curving things.

Arcing over and to the sides of a great figure's head. She couldn't see well through the plume of water that was coming from where the falls met the pool below. The figure was blurred by tens of thousands of airborne water droplets creating a cloud of mist that hung above the river.

The horns bobbed this way and that, and the animal shook, flinging water everywhere.

Her voice carried across the roar of the waterfall and the whistle of the wind: "Da di da da, and dee dee dee, I love the water, and the water loves me."

Whimsy ran for cover so that she wouldn't get soaked. She figured the water would be especially problematic for Flit. She found a good hiding spot in the ivy that grew along every inch of the empty cottage.

"Ba bi du da, and bi du be be, Standin' here splashin' 'neath the great oak tree."

The animal continued to hum to the beat of the made-up tune, but the water-flinging had

quieted enough to where Whimsy felt she could brave walking closer.

When she came to the top of a nearby rock, the animal's entirety came into view. The horns had been misleading, for what stood before Whimsy was anything but intimidating.

It was Mayflower Buffalo, who Whimsy remembered fondly. She may not have seen May in some time, but she knew her to be a dear friend of

Lady Porcupine's from way back when.

There'd even been tell that she was the one who'd wished for a new home for her quilled friend when the Wishweaver had still been around. That had been before Whimsy's time, though.

"Miss May?" Whimsy called.

"What, who's there?" came the deep voice of the wading buffalo. Whimsy ducked as water sprayed at her again.

"It's me... Whimsy."

"Whim. Is that you? I don't have my glasses on, sweet pea. I can't see you well." The water buffalo squinted in Whimsy's direction. Whimsy noticed the buffalo's glasses on a nearby rock and went to retrieve them for her. She carried the glasses up the side of the water buffalo's body, strapped with web to her back, and gently fixed them in front of Mayflower's eyes.

Whimsy backed away then, to the tip

of May's nose.

"Well, hello there, sweet pea. So nice to see you again. How long's it been?"

"It's been long enough for me to wonder where you'd gone to," Whimsy said.

"Whimsy, you know her?" Flit asked.

"Everyone knows Miss May. She's always been one of the elders in Weyburn. She sat on a council with my mom before she died, and with Lady Porcupine, too, among others."

"Have you seen Lady lately?"

"We saw her just yesterday! Enjoyed some of her famous crawler biscuits before we left, too," Whimsy said, remembering their sweet nutty flavor.

"How's she been?" Mayflower asked.

"Her roof had a leak, but I took care of it. I spun a plug that should hold her through the winter."

"That sure was sweet of you. I'm glad

to hear she's doing okay. I sure do miss her."

Mayflower walked them back toward her cottage.

"Why don't you go see her then?" Whimsy asked.

"Well, I'm sort of stuck where I'm at now."

"In this cottage?" Flit asked.

"The cottage. The bottom of the waterfall. A place most've forgotten about by now. Take your pick."

"Why are you here in the first place?" Whimsy asked.

"That's the better question to ask, isn't it?" Mayflower opened up the back door to the cottage and brought them inside.

It wasn't much—just a resting place for when May needed it, with some piles of grass she'd collected nearby for when she got hungry and a stove like Lady Porcupine's which was big enough to keep her warm on the coldest of winter nights.

May leaned down and placed Whimsy on top

of the pile of grass, and Whimsy found the perfect spot for Flit beside her. "I'll tell you a story while you're here, if you've the time for such things as stories."

"I've always got time for your stories," Whimsy said, settling in alongside Flit to listen. She'd heard a story or two told by May Buffalo, and knew that whatever she had worth telling was something that would be more than worth hearing.

May cleared her throat, settled herself in, and began, "It all started with a wish."

CHAPTER TEN

A TALE WORTH TELLING

"It was known throughout Weyburn that, should you want anything, anything at all, you just had to find the Wishweaver. When she was around, we all came to know her as Whisper. Whisper always told me how much she loved springtime. The winter snow melting away. Sweet flowers in bloom. Endless sunshine. And, best of all, the start of wish season.

"Whisper was happiest when she was weaving wishes, delighted to share her magic with others. 'Time to spin my webs,' she told me once. 'My darling wisps will be here soon!' Her webs tunneled. They swirled. They twisted and twirled. 'Wondrous,' some called them. 'Whimsical,' said others. 'Perfect,' said Whisper. And they were, for Whisper's webs caught every wisp.

"She filled the wisps with a sliver of her magic. All we wishers had to do was say what we wanted and set the wisp free. Whisper's magic took care of the rest. We all wanted something. Who doesn't?

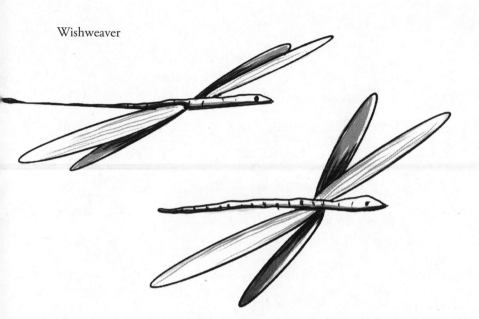

"When we found out our wishes could come true and that Whisper could help make that happen, we all sought her out. Friend and foe, small and large, we lined up together to see her and get one of her wish-granting, magic-filled wisps to answer our prayers.

"Miss
Woodpecker
wished that her
sister's broken
wing would

be healed. She broke open Whisper's webs, whispered what she wanted, and re-leased the wisp into the West Wind. The magic found her sister, and the broken wing was healed. It worked. Her wish was granted.

"Mr. Wolf followed. He wished that his pups would always have a dry bed to sleep in. No sooner did the wisp leave his paws, did he feel the pull of Whisper's magic, guiding him to an underground, abandoned den where his pups could grow into wolves in safety.

"My own first wish was that Lady Porcupine

would find a new home. Her last tree had fallen down once the roots had become rotten and could no longer hold the tree's weight. When I let go of my wisp, the path to her current home became clear. We followed the magic's tether, and there stood the hollowed-out tree, perfect for the home she had in mind. I rest easy knowing she was taken care of.

"We loved using wishes to help those dear to us. We were all so giving. It was truly magic to behold. Everyone working together. Making friends with our enemies. Loving our neighbors and wanting to see them happy. 'Seeing my magic used for such kindness is its own reward,' Whisper told many of us when we tried to pay her for the service she'd provided. She never asked for anything, but we brought what we could in thanks. None of us remember the exact moment it happened, but little by little, we stopped giving.

"We started wishing for ourselves, but were never truly happy. We still wanted more. We even stopped saying 'Thank you' and giving Whisper tokens of our appreciation for her kindness. Being able to have our wishes granted so easily made us greedy. It didn't take long before our wishes became ridiculous…"

******

"You mean like what Cricket wanted?" Whimsy asked. "Poor Cricket. I helped pull and tie her mop of hair back so she could walk—and see, for that matter. Her hair was growing out of control!"

"Out of control… that's a pretty good way of describing what happened," said May, thinking back.

"We heard the firefly got eaten!" Flit said.

"Who, Lennie?" May asked.

"Yep. The one that wanted to glow blue!" Flit

couldn't help but laugh at the thought.

"Poor Lennie. He didn't realize he'd attract the wrong kind of attention by making himself stand out so much. The frog that ate him apparently also had an affinity for the color blue. Would you like to know more of the story?"

"Yes, please!" Whimsy and Flit said together.

"Where was I?" Mayflower crinkled her eyebrows, trying her best to remember.

"Ridiculous wishes."

"Ah yes. You heard what happened to Cricket and Lennie, but you didn't hear what happened to me. You can imagine, perhaps, since I'm way down here, what I may have asked for.

"'I wish to wade in endless pools of water,' I said before letting my own wisp be taken by the West Wind. Even the West Wind had grown angered by all of the frivolous wishing going on.

"He worked so closely with Whisper to send wisps to her year after year for her wishweaving. He helped her magic get to the right places after each wish was made.

"This time around, it wasn't so much of a

magical pull that brought me here, to the foot of a roaring waterfall, so much as a push.

"The West Wind is strong and has a mind of his own when he wants to. I think my wish was the last straw for him. I regretted making it the minute I heard his loud roar of disapproval. Then, he swooped up all one thousand pounds of me, and away we flew.

"He brought me here to this abandoned cottage and dropped me in the water that I had wished to wade in endlessly.

"No sooner did I make my enormous splash than the West Wind

left me behind. With
him went any hope
I had of making my
way back to the home
I'd made in Weyburn.

I realized I would never get to see Lady Porcupine again, either, and that, I have found, is my biggest regret."

CHAPTER ELEVEN
A STORY UNFOLDS

"So, what happened next?" Whimsy asked.

"I've no idea. That's where my story ends. The West Wind brought me here, and ever since, here I've remained. Stuck at the bottom of a waterfall. Endless water to wade in, but no one to share it with. Destined to be alone, I suppose."

"Don't say that," Flit said, thinking of what his life would have been like without Whimsy.

"There's nothing to say you can't get back to Lady Porcupine again."

"Oh, my dear wisp, I've tried. Believe me, I've tried. I wanted nothing more than to spend the rest of my days with Lady. The fact that I wished for anything else still has me awake at night, but this is the choice I made, and I must accept that."

"It's not right," Whimsy replied, frustration in her voice over May's predicament.

"It may not be right, but it's what I asked for. I deserve no more or less than that."

Whimsy thought about what had happened after Mayflower Buffalo had been brought there, and more importantly, where the Wishweaver had gone. How had things gotten so messed up?

It didn't make sense.

The more Whimsy discovered, the more questions she had. How could the Wishweaver have let all of this happen? It didn't seem like the kind of wishing Whimsy would want to grant. And it still begged the question: What were they continuing the Wishweaver traditions for?

"Maybe things are better without the Wishweaver," Whimsy said.

Both Flit and Mayflower looked at Whimsy in surprise.

"Think about it, May. You're without Lady. Lennie's gone. Cricket's stuck in a net of her own hair. Is anyone happy now? Wouldn't you all have been better off if Whisper had never come to Weyburn?"

"You don't mean that, do you, Whimsy?" Flit asked.

Whimsy crossed a set of legs across her chest. "I mean every word." She couldn't help but be angry for the way things had turned out for the others. She loved helping people, and it seemed like all the Wishweaver had done was hurt them.

"I think we can go home now," Whimsy told Flit. "I don't think I need to see the Wishweaver tree anymore."

Whimsy stood up to leave and found herself being hoisted up onto the nose of Mayflower Buffalo.

"Now, you listen here, sweet pea. None of this is Whisper's fault. She wasn't the one doing the wishing."

"Yeah, but she could've not granted the wishes that were bad ones," Whimsy said.

"That's not how the wishing works, Whim. All Whisper did was share her magic with the rest of us. We were the ones who told that magic where

to go. The fault lies with the wisher, not the weav-
er. I hope you can understand that," May said.

"I'll try. I still don't know if I want to keep
going, though. Flit? What do you think?"

May brought Whimsy back down to her wisp

companion. Whimsy picked him back up in her front legs.

"Seems to me we still don't know everything," Flit said. "I think, before I take the next part in my own journey, I'd like to finish up this one. You've got me even more curious than I was before. Besides, I've always wanted to know what it felt like to be touched by Wishweaver magic. Maybe we'll meet another wisp who has."

"You've not much further to go," Mayflower said. "I'm certain you'll find the answers you seek along the way. I can take you as far as High Away Hill, and then the rest is up to you."

CHAPTER TWELVE

HIGH AWAY HILL

At the foot of High Away Hill, Whimsy understood why Mayflower couldn't carry them any further. The word 'hill' didn't really do it justice.

"Maybe High Away Mountain would've been a better name," Flit thought aloud.

"I was thinking the same thing," said Whimsy.

"There should be enough fallen trees for you to climb," May said. "It won't take long to cross over."

Mayflower placed them on top of a large log that had fallen down the hill a long time ago. Eye to eye, Whimsy walked over to rest her head against May's. "Thank you for telling us your story. I'll figure out the rest and come back to find you."

"I look forward to it, sweet pea. Until then."

******

It would've been tough for many of Weyburn's animal residents to climb High Away Hill, but for an orb spider like Whimsy, it was easy. She didn't have to go high up at all, with as much underbrush as there was to walk along.

They'd lost some of their afternoon travel time in getting stuck with the spiders and talking with Mayflower.

"We might still make it to the old oak by nightfall," Whimsy said as she jumped off the rough bark of another fallen tree and into the dry aspen leaves that sprinkled the ground.

"Watch it!" cried a muffled voice from beneath her. Whimsy hopped out of the way.

"Little help here?" asked a roly-poly who Whimsy had accidentally flipped onto his back.

"Sorry about that! I didn't see you there."

As Whimsy came down where the roly-poly could see her, he seemed to notice for the first time what had knocked into him.

"Ahhhhh! Don't eat meeee…" the voice trailed off as he popped into a ball. Whimsy picked the roly-poly up and tried to pry him open.

"I wouldn't wish of it," she said. It was an old saying that had caught on ever since the Wishweaver days.

Her reassurance put the little bug at ease, though, because he stopped fighting her and opened up enough to look at her.

"That's good to hear," the roly-poly said. A few moments passed while they stared blankly at each other. "You can put me down now."

"Yes, of course. And sorry about jumping on you. I really didn't see you there." Whimsy set the roly-poly down on the dry leaves.

"I've been told I'm easy to miss," he said, dusting himself off.

"Who told you that?" Flit asked.

"Everyone! Well, all the other roly-polys, at least. I'm pretty small, as I'm sure you've noticed."

"I hadn't noticed," Whimsy said, surveying the little creature more closely now.

"You didn't?" he asked.

"Nope! You look just the right size to me."

"Thanks Miss… I didn't catch your name."

"That's because I never said it." Whimsy smiled. "I'm Whimsy, and this is my friend, Flit."

"Hey," Flit said.

"I'm Rolland. Where're you two headed in such a hurry?"

"We're on our way to the Wishweaver tree. Do you know how much farther it is?"

"Miss Whisper's old place?" he asked.

Whimsy nodded.

"You've gone a tad off course, but I can get you going the right way, if you don't mind a roly-poly tagging along. I haven't visited there in a while. No time like today!"

"That would be great! Thanks for the help. You wouldn't believe the morning we've had."

"I always love a good adventure story!"

"Then I'll tell you ours on the way."

******

Whimsy had just finished telling Rolland about Mayflower Buffalo when they reached their final descent on the other side of High Away Hill. The ground got softer, and Whimsy took a moment to feel the rich soil beneath her legs.

"May was right. That wasn't as bad as I thought."

"You mean High Away Hill?" Rolland asked.

"Yeah."

"We were just lucky. There are some questionable things that hang out on High Away," said Rolland.

"Like you?" Flit asked.

"Ha, ha. Very funny. Seriously, though, that's

not the place to be at night."

"Glad we made it through while the sun was still out then," Whimsy said.

"We're not out of the woods yet. We need to make it to the oak tree by sunset."

CHAPTER THIRTEEN
SUNSET

Everything seemed against them.

There were numerous downed trees in their path, which they had no choice but to climb. Flit was back to gripping onto Whimsy's shoulder so that she had all of her legs free to climb. Rolland was able to climb on the rough bark, too, but there were several places where even he needed Whimsy to carry him.

"Thanks, Whimsy. Rolys are terrible climbers. And you can forget about climbing upside-down! We have no stick to our feet." Rolland did a little tap dance to illustrate the feet he was talking about.

Whimsy laughed. "The benefits of being a spider, I guess."

The cool breeze pushed through the hairs on Whimsy's body and she shivered. The cooler temperature meant they were running out of time. The forest had darkened so gradually, their eyes must have adjusted without them realizing they were losing the daylight.

"Oh no!" Flit said. "Look!"

He pointed to the rising moon. The skies were pink where the sun made its fast descent toward the horizon.

"There's no way we'll

get to the Wishweaver tree in time," Rolland said.

"What do we do now?" asked Whimsy.

"We have to hide," Rolland said.

They searched the grounds for a dark hole to climb into. The ground had turned rocky, though. The rocks lay so densely on top of each other, Whimsy couldn't find a single cavern within them to sleep in for the night. The rocks were endless. There were no trees overhead to hide them, either.

There were two sounds that came to them on the wind, sending chills up Whimsy's back. One thing, she knew for certain. "The night animals are waking up!" she said, fear getting the better of her. "What now?"

"Run!" Rolland shouted.

They ran.

They ran as fast as they could, but the size of the rocks made them feel like the ground was going in the opposite direction. It slowed down their

progress and kept
them vulnerable.

Whimsy picked
up Rolland with one
leg and made sure Flit was
secure in the crook of another. She was
the fastest runner among them, and if
anyone could get them out of this mess,
she knew it would be her.

She could see the trees up ahead.
There was sure to be a place to hide in the
brush. "Almost there… I think we're going
to make it," Whimsy said, panting.

But the sound of wingbeats rose behind them.
Whimsy kept running, too afraid to stop.

"Whoooo, hooooooooo…" was the last thing
Whimsy heard before the rocks fell away beneath
her feet.

CHAPTER FOURTEEN
NIGHT ANIMALS

Whimsy looked down. She watched the trees zoom past her. She smelled mint and eucalyptus in the air. She felt the talons trapping her and her companions. There was nowhere to go now.

"This must be what bugs feel like when they're caught in our webs," she said thoughtfully. "Perhaps this is how it was meant to be."

"Have you been knocked on the head, Whim?" Flit asked. "Snap out of it!"

"Huh?" she asked.

"We just have to think," said Rolland. "What caught us?"

They all looked up into the plumed white feathers of their captor. A woodland owl.

"He definitely plans to eat us," Whimsy said. "This isn't good."

"Do you have anything he might want?" Rolland wondered aloud.

"You mean besides us for dinner?" Flit asked.

"He probably won't eat you, Flit. You aren't really edible," Whimsy said.

"True, but that doesn't help you two any. Wait. I just thought of something," Flit said, remembering.

"What?" Rolland asked.

"What is it?" Whimsy asked.

"Biscuits," Flit answered.

"Biscuits?" Whimsy asked. Then she, too, remembered. "Biscuits! That's it!"

"I'm confused," Rolland said with a frown and a furrowed brow.

"In my pack, I still have some of Lady Porcupine's crawler biscuits! She did say they might come in handy."

"I doubt this is what she had in mind," Flit said.

******

The owl took them to a place where Whimsy thought the sun was shining once more. It was a tree so orange and yellow that even the night sky couldn't dampen its brilliance. Atop one of the high-reaching branches, the owl landed. He walked them into the hollowed-out trunk where he set them by the stove.

"Don't even think about escaping," the owl said, pointing his wing at the doorway. He called out, "We're having roly-spider stew for dinner, Peanut. With a dried seed on top!"

Flit swallowed. "Dried seed?"

"We?" Rolland asked.

"Peanut?" Whimsy whispered.

"Oh, how lovely, Pie. Told you it was a good night for hunting!"

A second owl came up from the stairs that led down deeper into the tree. Peanut was the smaller of the two, but only by a feather. She checked the stove where a pot of water sat boiling. Satisfied at the temperature, she looked over at Whimsy and the others.

"That's it, Pie?" she asked him. "They're a bit small for us to share, don't you think?"

"I can go out and get more if you want." Pie ducked his head down, upset about having disappointed Peanut.

"If you want to eat tonight, too, I'd say you'd

better hurry!"

Pie took off through the doorway and back out into the night to find more spiders and roly-polys to add to the stew.

"Care to chat while we wait for silly ole Pie?" Peanut asked, nestling down beside them.

Whimsy thought it odd that Peanut wanted to talk to her food, but knew better than to ask. She had to think fast.

"We'd love to chat! I was wondering how your tree stays such pretty colors while the others are only green."

"Oh, that was Pie. He knows how much I love autumn colors, so he used his last wish to ask that our cottonwood tree stay those fiery colors year-round. Beautiful, aren't they?" Peanut asked, admiring the leaves of her cottonwood tree.

"Stunning," Whimsy said. "You mentioned his 'last wish'?"

"From Whisper. You know, the Wishweaver?"

"Oh, yes. Do you know what happened to her?" Whimsy asked, trying to keep Peanut's mind off of how sweet she might taste in the roly-spider stew.

"There's been tell around Weyburn that she died. They say the reason no other Wishweaver took her place was because she'd used up her last bit of magic granting silly wishes. Without enough magic to pass to another, the Wishweaver line dies out, too.

"It's all rather sad if you think about it. Not sure I would've let Pie ask for the cottonwood leaves to stay autumn colors if I'd known that was going to be our last wish." Peanut looked out at the leaves again, watching them sway in the night air.

"What would your wish have been instead?" Rolland asked.

"Not sure, really," said Peanut. "Perhaps something that could've helped Pie and I more. Endless food or... or... ooh, maybe more of Lady Porcupine's crawler biscuits. We haven't had enough energy to make our way out to that part of Weyburn in quite some time."

And there it was.

The weight of the biscuits in Whimsy's pack lay heavy on her back. "What if I could grant one of your wishes? Would you let us go?"

"Let you go? I'd do one better than that! I'd bring you wherever you wanted to go. I haven't had a decent meal since Pie lost most of his eyesight. He can't tell a branch from a snake on his best night. I'm surprised he even managed to get you lot."

"I have some of Lady's crawler biscuits in my bag. I'll give you six of them if you'll take the three of us to the Wishweaver Oak," Whimsy said, pulling her pack down from her back and untying the top. The smell of the crawler biscuits wafted into the room and Peanut's eyes went wide.

"Gimme, gimme, gimme," Peanut said, losing all sense.

Whimsy held up two of her front legs to stop the owl from rushing into her.

"I'll give you three now since I know you're hungry. I'm guessing you'll need your strength to fly us to the oak tree. When you get us there, you can have the other three. What do you say?"

Flit and Rolland looked from Whimsy to

Peanut and back again. They made a silent agreement not to say anything, not when they were very close to getting what they all wanted.

"I say, if you give me three of those biscuits now, I'll get you where you need to go. I have one request of you, though."

"What's that?" Whimsy asked.

"Don't tell Pie if you see him again." Peanut winked at them.

"It's our little secret," Whimsy said, handing over the first half of the crawler biscuits.

Peanut gobbled a biscuit. "Mmmmmm...." She scarfed down another. "Delicious!" The last biscuit made its way into her beak. "What perfect craftsmanship," Peanut said with biscuit in her mouth. "Lady outdid herself this time. Best cook in Weyburn."

"I agree," Whimsy said with a smile.

Peanut turned her back to Whimsy, Rolland, and Flit, still chewing her last biscuit, and pointed a wing to her back, gesturing for them to climb on.

Whimsy lifted her friends to hold them tight, climbed atop the woodland owl, and away they flew.

CHAPTER FIFTEEN
EYES OPEN

Whimsy couldn't look down. She wouldn't.

It was tough enough knowing how high up they were, riding on Peanut's back, but it would be entirely different seeing it with her own eyes. All eight of them.

Nope.

Whimsy was determined not to look.

"Whimsy, you've gotta see this!" Flit called.

"There's nothing like it!" cried Rolland. "Weeeeeeeeeeeeee… we're flying!" Peanut's wings flapped to a steady rhythm. Every so often, she paused to glide for a bit.

It was a comfortable ride, but one Whimsy wished they didn't have to take. "I'm good," Whimsy said. "You two go ahead."

"Oh, come on, Whimsy, when are we going to get another chance like this?" Rolland asked.

She felt Flit brush his wispy arms against her closed eyelids. Rolland grasped onto her leg that held him even tighter.

Her friends were with her. She was safe.

She wasn't alone.

Whimsy took a deep breath and opened her eyes.

CHAPTER SIXTEEN
WEYBURN FROM ABOVE

The view was extraordinary!

Time froze when you were up so high. Every bad thing that had happened on their journey thus far melted away with the passing clouds.

Weyburn from above was a sight to behold. Firefly light illuminated every inch of the landscape while the little flyers came out to play in the darkness. They zipped this way and that. Their dancing was a light show like no other Whimsy had ever seen.

Even the sounds intrigued her.

The hooting of Peanut's relations. The howling of wolves at the glowing moon overhead.

The West Wind whipping his way through the cattails and reeds, knocking them together, to make a beautiful percussion.

Through it all, the grasshoppers played their nightly violin song while the frogs croaked their own melody.

From up high, Whimsy could see that all of the nocturnal creatures worked together, however unintentionally, to turn Weyburn at night into a place filled with as much liveliness as there was during the daytime.

"It really is magical," Whimsy said.

"We told you!" Flit said, shouting above the sounds of Peanut's flapping wings.

"Oh, look!" Whimsy said, pointing below. "It's where Pie found us."

The rocks were clearly visible now, with their pale glow and the light reflecting from the full moon.

Peanut kept going. It seemed that Whimsy, Rolland,

and Flit had been headed in the right direction when Pie had caught them. Rolland was right.

He did know the way.
Lucky for them,
they'd managed
a ride that could
get them to the
Wishweaver
tree faster
than they ever
could have
gotten there
on foot.
"Nearly there!"
Peanut called back to
them. "The Wishweaver Oak is just up ahead!"
Whimsy and the others looked
forward. There was a dark area
where the firefly light stopped.

"I hope we're not going in there," Whimsy whispered to her friends.

"Me, too," Flit said.

Rolland just held on tighter.

"You all aren't afraid of the dark, are you?" Peanut asked with a laugh.

"Of course not!" Whimsy said. She was a spider, after all. They loved nighttime. But there was something about the darkness ahead that was unnerving.

It felt like a black hole pulling them into an abyss. They could easily be lost, or worse, forgotten, in a place like that. Whimsy shook away her negative thoughts.

She'd have to be brave for all of them because they were indeed heading straight into the darkness beyond.

CHAPTER SEVENTEEN
THE DARKNESS BEYOND

All spiders can see at night. In fact, usually they prefer it.

Here, in the darkness beyond, on the outskirts of Weyburn, Whimsy felt the heaviness of the shadows. Even the air felt thick with them.

No fireflies were here to lend their glow. Even

the moonlight was blocked out by the thick over-growth of trees.

"I have a bad feeling about this," Flit said. "Maybe this wasn't such a good idea."

"Oh, don't be such a wisp," Whimsy said with a sheepish smile.

"What's that supposed to mean?" Flit asked, frowning at her.

"I have no clue."

He couldn't help but laugh.

"Just think, the sun will be out soon. I'm sure everything will look different in the daylight."

"Different doesn't always mean better, or so the other roly-polys have told me," Rolland said.

"You can't listen to them! Look, everyone said I wasn't a spider because I don't like high places. Now, look at me! Can't get much higher than riding on the back of a flying owl, can you?" Whimsy asked.

"True enough," Rolland said. "I'll try my best to ignore them. Still, I hope you're right about seeing this place in the daytime. But first we have to last the night."

******

The Wishweaver tree stood just up ahead. It was wider than it was tall. To Whimsy, it seemed to have given up growing towards the sky and instead shot its branches out, twisting and twirling, back toward the ground.

To say
the tree
was gnarled
didn't quite
describe this
otherworldly
being.
It was by
far the most
magnificent
thing
Whimsy had
ever seen.

"Is that the
Wishweaver
tree?" she
called up to
Peanut.
"The one
and only!"
Peanut said.
"Can you feel
the magic,
Flit?" Whimsy
asked,

feeling the energy coursing through the air.

"What magic?" he asked.

The familiar tingling prickled along Whimsy's forehead as they drew closer. She reached a leg up to see if there was something there.

The smooth place between her eyes was as it had always been.

Only my imagination. Or perhaps the wind.

"We're coming in for a landing. Hold on tight!" Peanut yelled.

Whimsy gripped the soft feathers at the base of Peanut's neck. Boy, was she glad she did…

CHAPTER EIGHTEEN
WEBS

Peanut misjudged her landing and flew them smack dab into an oak branch instead of landing gracefully on top of it.

Once again, they were falling. It seemed to be an unfortunate theme on this journey. Peanut wasn't moving as she fell.

Whimsy had only enough time to briefly worry about the state she was in before they hit

the ground. Peanut's out-
stretched wings had helped
slow their fall, and her body provided the needed cushion for the rest of
them.

Whimsy climbed down off Peanut's back and
put Rolland on the ground beside her. The owl
wasn't moving.

"Is she okay?" Rolland asked, climbing onto
Peanut's face, which seemed twisted a little too
much to one side.

"I'm not sure," Whimsy said. She walked over

to where Rolland was poking the lifeless owl and lay her ear to Peanut's neck. A quiet thumping pushed back at her. A faint heartbeat. "She's alive, but only just."

"What do we do?" Flit asked.

Whimsy looked around, but there was no one there to help her. She was on her own in this.

Wait. Didn't Lin Beaver mention something about helping rebuild a torn-down beaver dam near the Wishweaver tree?

"That's it!" Whimsy said.

"What's it?" Flit asked.

"We need to find the river again. There'll be someone there who can help us. I hate to leave her here alone, though…"

"I'll go," Rolland said. "I know this area like the back of my shell. The river isn't far. See what you can do for Peanut while I'm gone."

Rolland took off into the bushes, and Whimsy and Flit were alone.

"We need to find some way to lift her up. I

can't tell how badly she's hurt," Whimsy said.

"Think you can build a web?" Flit asked.

"How's a web going to help?" Whimsy wondered.

"Well, you use webs to hold us wisps up while we wait to be planted, right?"

"Yeah… so?"

"So, maybe you can do the same for Peanut."

"It's worth a try."

"Wait, why are we even helping her?" Flit thought aloud. "Wasn't she going to eat us? Roly-spider stew with a seed on top, remember?"

"Flit, that's not important anymore. She needs our help. I can't stand by and watch her hurt."

"Suit yourself. Let me know if there's anything I can do," Flit said, with a hint of doubt in his voice.

"There is something you can do!"

"There is?" Flit perked up.

"You can be my lookout."

"Lookout for what?" he asked.

"Night animals."

"I'm on it!"

Whimsy climbed up the Wishweaver tree to find a good spot for Flit to stand as lookout.

She found it in the bend of a branch. Then, without fear, Whimsy felt the breeze to see where she'd need to begin spinning. She moved into position on the underside of the tree branch and let her silk go. It caught the breeze, which brought the strand gently back over to the tree trunk, where it held fast.

Like a tightrope walker, Whimsy made her way to the other side and began building her web.

It didn't need to be a big one. Just enough for Flit to stick to.

Whimsy was better at spinning webs than she'd thought. Her webs had a certain flare to them, a design that she hadn't seen the other spiders make when they spun their own. She figured it was because she was doing it wrong, but either way, her web would hold Flit. She had no doubt about that.

"I'm good," Flit said, nestled against the sticky spider silk. "Go on and build Peanut's web now."

Whimsy climbed onto another branch below where Flit hung looking this way and that.

She could see how serious he was taking the job he'd been tasked with.

Whimsy found another good spot, where she felt the next web needed to start, and so she once again put a leg out to feel the wind. She waited for the current of air to move at just the right angle to grab her thread. As soon as she felt it, Whimsy began.

She worked at a speed that would have amazed even the best spinners. Whimsy found that spinning webs did indeed come as naturally to her as planting wisps. It felt right.

She walked across the spider silk with ease. She hung upside down. She swung from her web knowing it would hold her. Her fear had left her.

Whimsy's web was as whimsical as her name suggested. It even had zigzags for added strength. Peanut would be the heaviest thing Whimsy, or any of the spiders, had ever tried to catch.

There were swirls. Twirls. Dips. Bends. Funnels. Even pointed oval shapes that gave the appearance of eyes looking outward.

The web wasn't a single layer of thickness. It couldn't be if it was going to support Peanut and give her a soft place to lie. Every layer of webbing would be just what the owl needed to hold true and safe while Whimsy figured out if there was anything else wrong with her besides a blow to the head.

"Perfect," Whimsy said.

"Do you see anyone?" Whimsy called up to Flit.

"It's a quiet night," Flit called back down to her.

"Not even Rolland?"

"Nope!"

"Now, what do I do?" Whimsy asked herself. "How am I going to get Peanut onto my web? She's so much bigger than I am! I can't just lift her."

"There's something coming!" Flit yelled. "Hide!"

CHAPTER NINETEEN
COMPANY

Whimsy noticed there was a small cave made by the curve of Peanut's wing and she ran inside it, huddling in the shadows.

The nearby ferns began to move. Whimsy watched them. She waited.

"This way," came a familiar voice.

Rolland walked up onto a boulder, waving someone forward.

The rustling behind him grew
louder. It sounded like something was
being dragged along the dried leaves
covering every inch of the ground.

"Who did he bring?"
Whimsy whispered,
staying in her hiding
spot while she
watched.

Whimsy saw the beavers first. Lin Beaver was at the front of the group. Then the lightning bugs flew in, providing their light.

They must have been working together to rebuild the dam, Whimsy thought. It was nice to see the creatures in Weyburn working together even when they didn't have to.

Then came a great, "Hoooo, hooo, hooo!"

Whimsy looked down at Peanut, who was still unmoving except for her chest rising and falling with each breath.

"Where's my Peanut? Let me see her! Let me see her!"

Whimsy came out from under Peanut's wing.

Pie hopped over to where Peanut lay. He shook his head back and forth. "My sweet pea. My sweet pea."

Rolland walked over to Whimsy, explaining, "Pie came looking for Peanut, and we picked him up on our way back."

Whimsy nodded. "We need to see if she's hurt anywhere else," Whimsy said, meeting Pie head-on.

"Huh, who's there?" Pie squinted to get a better look at Whimsy, who now stood atop Peanut's back.

"You! Did you do this to my Peanut?" he asked, anger seeping into his voice.

"I'm not sure what happened. We made a deal with her to take us here and I would give her crawler biscuits in my pack from Lady Porcupine." Whimsy cursed herself for breaking her promise to Peanut about not telling Pie. Maybe he won't remember, Whimsy thought.

"You've got Lady's biscuits!"

"That's beside the point. The deal was she'd get another three after bringing us here. We almost landed on the branch, but somehow ran straight into it instead."

"I keep telling Peanut to let me do the flyin'. Why don't she listen? I can do the hunting. You don't have to see too well to hunt."

"What's wrong with her?" Whimsy asked, Rolland still at her side. The rest of the beavers circled around to listen.

"Peanut's great at flying, but not
so great at landing these days.

She never seems to land where
she aims to. This isn't the first
time she's run into a branch,"
Pie said.

"Can you help me get her into my web so I can have a look at her?" Whimsy asked.

"I'll help!" Lin Beaver stepped forward. "Hey, Whim. Good to see ya!"

"You, too, Lin." Whimsy smiled.

"We'll help, too!"

"'Course I'll help!" Pie said.

It took every one of them to lift Peanut up.

Whimsy didn't want to make things worse if Peanut had broken something this time around, so they had to be careful. Peanut was placed on the web with her wings fully outstretched. Not a feather was out of place.

Now Whimsy could look at her.

Peanut hadn't just hit the branch. Whimsy had been worried about that.

If she'd just been knocked out from the impact, she probably would've come to by now. No, Peanut was hurt bad.

A piece of the Wishweaver tree branch had broken off on impact and was sticking out from

Peanut's wing. It appeared to be a shallow wound, upon closer inspection, but Whimsy worried what would happen when they removed the wood.

Either way, it needed to come out.

"What now?" asked Pie, a hitch in his voice.

"I need a needle," Whimsy announced.

"A need—" Pie didn't finish his sentence. The thought of needles sent him falling backward in a dead faint.

"I've got you covered!" said Lin.

The beaver escaped into the bushes. Whimsy watched, wondering what Lin could be doing in there.

"Aha!" Whimsy heard. "Bingo!"

Back out of the bushes, Lin walked with a small stick coming out either side of her mouth.

Her two front teeth shone in the firefly light, and it looked to Whimsy like she was very pleased with herself.

Lin walked up beside Whimsy and scrunched down. "Hang on," she said, pulling the stick from her mouth. "Only be a moment."

Wood shavings flew.

It was fun watching beavers do what they did best. Gnawing.

Whimsy supposed they each had their own hidden talents. It seemed like her own was spinning webs.

"There. Done." Lin handed a perfectly carved wooden needle over to Whimsy.

Whimsy spun a length of silk and tied off the end. She'd have to work quickly so that Peanut didn't lose too much blood.

"Who can pull the branch out?" Whimsy asked.

"What? What happened?" Pie rolled upright. "Did you say something?" He looked to Whimsy.

"I asked if anyone could pull the branch from Peanut's wing."

"I'll do it," Pie said.

"Okay, get ready... steady..." Whimsy began. Pie grabbed hold of the branch. "Now!" He yanked the branch from Peanut's wing, and Whimsy moved in a blur.

She was as fast at mending as she was at spinning webs.

With needle and spider silk thread, Whimsy stitched. With eight legs to work with, she could easily close the hole and stitch it shut without assistance. In a feverish hurry, Whimsy worked while everyone watched.

When she'd finished the front end, she checked the back. The branch hadn't gone straight through.

"Done," she said.

Pie hopped over to survey Whimsy's handiwork. He had to move in close to see it well. "Wow!" he said.

"Silly ole Pie," came a soft voice from beneath him.

"Peanut? That you, sweet pea? You alright?"

"Hungry," she said, opening her eyes. She looked over at Whimsy. "Do I still get those three more crawler biscuits?"

Whimsy had already pulled them from her bag. "They're right here." She handed them to Peanut, who was now lounging in the hammock of spider silk.

"You planning to share those, Peanut?" Pie asked.

She squinted one eye at him, then rolled them both with a shrug. "I suppose."

CHAPTER TWENTY
THE WISHWEAVER OAK

Lin was the last to leave.

"You sure you don't want me to take you back?" she asked. "You've seen the tree. Isn't that enough, Whim?"

"I still feel like there's more questions to be answered here. I'll be back as soon as I've figured

things out,"
Whimsy said,
looking up into
the reaches of the
Wishweaver Oak.

"Suit yourself. Wait
til Edmund hears about
the webs his little sister can
spin! Who-wee! The look on
his face will be priceless. See ya!"
Lin called, turning her paddle tail
to them and walking back the way
she'd come.

Whimsy hadn't even noticed
that the sky was changing col-
or. It wasn't black anymore,
and a pale blue was seeping
through. The daylight was finally coming.

"We made it through the
night," Whimsy told Rolland.

"We certainly did! Eventful as always," Rolland said.

"Shall we rest before we explore some more?" Whimsy asked through a yawn.

"Maybe we can find a nice place to rest inside?" Flit called down, still securely fastened to his lookout point. "Then I won't have to contend with blowing away while I close my eyes for a bit."

"Good point," Rolland said.

Whimsy scooped Rolland up and climbed up to retrieve Flit before going higher.

******

Whimsy climbed up to the branch where Peanut had tried but epically failed to land.

She passed a few puffy, pale mushrooms sticking from the side of the tree along the way. Whimsy remembered being told that they'd be there, helping her know she had made it to the right place.

When she crested the round edge and stood at the top, she could see why Peanut had chosen this particular branch.

An arcing door stood where the branch grew from the tree trunk. It wasn't large, but was big enough for a spider and anything smaller to crawl through. The door was lighter in color than the rest of the tree bark, as though it was made of wood that had been taken from a different tree. Dark hinges stood out on the left side and there was a great brass doorknob with a pointed oval shape etched into its face.

The shape looked familiar.

"Should we knock?" Whimsy asked.

"Whisper's gone. There'll be no one there to answer," Rolland said matter-of-factly.

"Good point." Whimsy tried the knob.

Locked.

"Great, now that we've come all this way," said Flit.

Whimsy eyed the rectangle of brass that framed the doorknob. To her surprise, she found there was, in fact, a keyhole.

There was a small roof—more of an overhang—built above the entryway. There were shingles made from more scraps of wood. Whimsy felt above for the key and came away empty-handed.

"Whim, what're you doing?" Flit asked.

"Where there's a keyhole, there's a key. We just need to find it."

She looked off to the right and saw the mushrooms she'd passed on her way up the Wishweaver Oak. From this vantage point, she realized they weren't just any ole fungi. These were more like flat-topped stepping stones leading to the front door. They felt very welcoming to her, like Whisper must have enjoyed company.

Whisper wouldn't have needed mushrooms to get to her own front door. She would have grown them to help others find her.

Whimsy continued her search.

"I'll help," Rolland said. So long as the tree had rough bark, he could climb it. He just had to be very careful not to go upside down.

Rolland climbed.

Whimsy walked around using the mushroom steps.

Flit watched from Whimsy's shoulder, where he held on tight.

As they inspected the Wishweaver Oak for its hidden key—if there was one to be found—Whimsy also looked for answers.

She looked up, and noticed reflecting light shining off the paned glass of a window.

"Hey, Rolland!" she called out to the roly-poly who was on the other side of the tree.

"Did you find something?" he asked.

"Come here and I'll show you!" Whimsy climbed higher, leaving the mushroom stairs behind.

Rolland circled back around to where Whimsy now stood peering inside the hollow tree. She used a leg to wipe a clean circle so they could get a better look.

"What do you see?" Rolland asked.

Whimsy took for granted how well she stuck to the sides of things. Poor Rolland was hanging on for dear life. She grabbed her friend so he could see for himself. "Look how tidy it is inside."

"There's nothing wrong with being tidy," Rolland said, puffing up his little chest. "I may love to soak in cool, damp places, but I also love keeping a tidy house."

"Yeah, but don't you think it's a little too clean?"

"Nope. Can't be too clean," Rolland said.

"I don't think you get what Whimsy's saying," said Flit. "It looks like it's being lived in, as in currently lived in. Look!" Flit said, pointing to the fireplace that appeared to still hold a glowing ember or two.

"Oh, I see what you mean." Rolland squished his face against the glass. "Look over there on the couch!"

There was indeed a couch that looked well rested upon with patches sewn in several places to

keep the stuffing in. What Rolland was pointing to, however, was the blanket that rested on top of it. The blanket was shoved to the side as though whoever had been beneath its comfort had been in a rush to get up.

"Huh," Whimsy said, crinkling her nose. "Maybe someone decided to live here since nobody else was? It's not the first time I've seen abandoned homes taken over by somebody else.

Maybe they needed a place to stay for a while that was safe. After what we've just been through, can you blame them?"

"No. Still, where did they go?" Flit asked. There was no movement to be seen.

"Let's keep looking," Whimsy suggested.

Whimsy was sure there was more to be found. She had to believe they hadn't come all this way to face a locked door and no answers.

A key was still out there.

It has to be, Whimsy hoped.

And she intended to find it.

CHAPTER TWENTY-ONE
THINGS HIDDEN

The sense of magic that flowed around this place was still present. Whimsy could feel it. It felt like a soft humming that could sting as quickly as it could soothe.

She was the only one, though, who noticed, so she kept it to herself. She didn't want Rolland and Flit to think she was crazy or something.

Once Whimsy and the others had looked at

just about every inch of the trunk, they followed the branches that led to the ground and those that led to the skies, all to see if what they needed could be found among them.

Rolland took off on his own again since two looking was always better than one.

"This is hopeless," Flit said, resting his seedy head on her shoulder. "I'm so tired! I just want to sleep already."

"I know, Flit. Me, too. Here." Whimsy brought him down to cradle him beneath the warmth of her fur. "Why don't you rest now? I'll keep you warm and I'll wake you if I find anything."

With a heavy sigh, snuggled up close against Whimsy, Flit fell fast asleep. She laughed when she realized for the first time that wisps could actually snore.

He really must be tired, she thought.

With Flit asleep, Whimsy decided to stop for a moment, too. She needed clarity, and it felt as though their efforts were running them in circles.

She stopped all of her movement: the searching, the wanting, the waiting.

When her world became about one thing and one thing only, a basic need to sleep, the magic found her.

An image flooded her mind. A key.

A hidden location, where most would never think to look.

Whimsy's eyes shot open and she ran, with a startled, bleary-eyed Flit in her arms, as fast as her six available legs could carry her. She snaked up the trunk, skipping with glee over the heads of a few mushrooms before gripping the rough bark once again.

Up and up she climbed.

"Rolland! Where are you?" Whimsy cried.

"Here at the front door," came a sleepy voice.

Whimsy was already headed that way, and so she reached him in no time.

"I'm sorry, Whimsy," the roly-poly said, lying beneath the overhang, "I was just so tired." Rolland rubbed the sleep from his eyes.

"It's okay. Come with me!" Whimsy picked him up, knowing it would be faster this way, and, with a smile on her face, she went higher.

There was a branch that shot toward the west. It was the only one pointed straight and true.

"They always said around Weyburn that the Wishweaver and the West Wind worked together, didn't they?"

Flit and Rolland nodded.

"Well, a thought popped into my head—an image really, of a branch I remember seeing earlier when we were searching. It seemed odd to me at the time, that it was the only straight branch out of all of them. Then, when I closed my eyes for a second, there it was again."

They reached the top, where the sky opened up and they had a magnificent view of the sun rising in the east. The day was looking to promise many things.

Whimsy saw the notch in the wood this time because she knew where to look.

She reached the slender tip of one leg beneath it and lifted up. A small sliver of wood gave way to reveal a hollowed-out area beneath.

The sun bounced off the metal hidden inside. It was a single brass key.

CHAPTER TWENTY-TWO
A KEY AND A LOCK

The minute, the very second that Whimsy picked up the key, she knew. If answers were what she sought, she was holding them.

"Let's see where this key takes us," Whimsy said.

"Lead the way," Rolland said, not hiding his own excitement.

The journey there had felt so long and

treacherous, but somehow it was all worth it at long last. At least, that's what they all hoped.

They were going to find out more about Weyburn.

But, more important than that, they hoped to find out about Whisper and what had really happened to her.

As she approached the door, Whimsy found it was already open a crack. "What the..." she whispered.

"Maybe whoever's been staying here left in a hurry while we were occupied looking for that key." Flit was always the rational one, which made Whimsy smile, seeing as he was also the most delicate.

"Let's try the key anyway, just to see if we have the right one." Whimsy tested the key in the lock and found that... it didn't fit. "How is that possible?"

"Who knows? Nothing about our way here has made any sense," Rolland said.

Whimsy set the roly-poly down just beyond the door. She reached up to grab her pack that still held the last two crawler biscuits. She thought about eating them—she was hungry, after all—but also realized Lady Porcupine had been right. They'd come in handy along the way.

They had stopped them from being eaten by Peanut and Pie, hadn't they?

She decided to save them.

Into her bag went the key. It was another question to be answered, but that's what they were there for.

It has to mean something. I'm going to figure out just what that is.

Whimsy and Flit came in to join Rolland and closed the door behind them. "Time to figure things out," Whimsy said.

"Let's split up and look around." Rolland scurried away.

Flit looked at Whimsy. "Mind if I tag along?"

Whimsy giggled. "Oh, right. I forgot."

"You always do." Flit had sounded a bit sad as he'd spoken.

"Oh, come on. You have so much to say, I forget you can't move unless the wind blows."

"Yeah, and then I don't have any control where I go!"

"Come on, Flit. Let's be happy! This is exciting, don't ya think?"

"You're right. Hey, Whim." Flit pointed to a newspaper wedged between the cushions of the couch they'd seen through the window.

Whimsy grabbed it and took a look. It was *The Weyburn Whistler*, their daily newspaper. She expected the date would read several years prior, but found it had been printed only the day before.

She scratched her head. "Does that say what I think it says?" Whimsy pointed to the date at the upper left corner of the front page.

"Sure does! Someone's definitely been staying here. I'm going to bet it was the same someone who left in such a hurry!"

Whimsy knew Flit was right.

"Look, the paper talks about the Redwood Dam the beavers are working on. It even mentions Lin and her mother Maybelle Beaver, and how they've been there every night working straight through to get the dam rebuilt."

"Whimsy, you're getting caught up in details again. Let's keep looking," Flit said.

"Right." Whimsy closed the paper and began to set it back down on the couch.

"Wait!" Flit said. "There."

Where Flit pointed was a small article on the back of the paper. It was a weekly post called "Unanswered Wishes."

The article began separating from the rest of the paper on three of the four sides. Whimsy held it up and realized that whoever had been staying there had been cutting this particular article out.

She looked to the side table where a small pair of scissors lay, still open… as though whoever had left them there had done so mid-cut.

"It's a list," Whimsy said. "A list of all the things everyone in Weyburn would wish for if Whisper was still around:

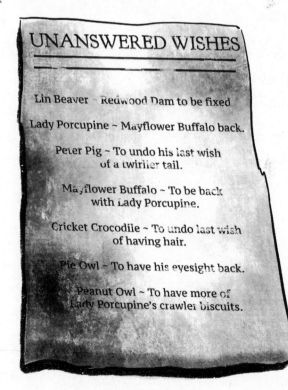

UNANSWERED WISHES

Lin Beaver ~ Redwood Dam to be fixed

Lady Porcupine ~ Mayflower Buffalo back.

Peter Pig ~ To undo his last wish of a twirlier tail.

Mayflower Buffalo ~ To be back with Lady Porcupine.

Cricket Crocodile ~ To undo last wish of having hair.

Pie Owl ~ To have his eyesight back.

Peanut Owl ~ To have more of Lady Porcupine's crawler biscuits.

Whimsy laughed at the last one. "Peanut does really love those biscuits, doesn't she?"

"Lucky for us!"

"What a great way for some of the wishes to be granted," Whimsy said, setting down the paper.

"What do you mean?" Flit asked.

"Some of the wishes can be granted by others in Weyburn. They don't need a Wishweaver to grant them."

"That's true. Sad, though. There are still some that will go unanswered."

"There always will be," Whimsy said. It was just a fact of life.

"Where to next?" Flit asked.

"Hey, Whimsy, check this out!" they heard Rolland call from somewhere below the floorboards.

"Rolland? Where are you?"

"There's a trapdoor beneath the corner rug. Come check this out!"

It wasn't difficult to spot the rug Rolland was

talking about since he had already skootched it back to get underneath.

She noticed a knot in the wood that had fallen away, leaving a hole through which Rolland had undoubtedly climbed.

Whimsy, on the other hand, was much too big to fit through it, so she lifted the handle and found that it, too, was locked.

"It's locked!" Whimsy called through the hole.

"Did you try the key?" Rolland suggested.

The key!

CHAPTER TWENTY-THREE
UNANSWERED WISHES

Whimsy fit the key inside the lock and turned.

Click.

The door swung open.

"It worked!" Whimsy said, doing a silly little dance.

"Watch it!" Flit called, holding on for dear life.

Whimsy laughed wholeheartedly. She was so excited to see what Rolland had found.

She dove in.

She expected to land on more hard wood, but instead found herself on a soft, sticky material she instantly knew to be spider webs. Whimsy looked around. This small room below the floorboards was covered in webs.

The webs themselves were unique. Much like her own, but also different. These had different designs and patterns she'd never seen, but among them was that same, familiar pointed oval that she made in her own webs. It was very curious to feel a familiarity in another spider's webs, connecting to her own.

Whimsy noticed these webs were created to hold boxes that lined every wall. She wondered what was inside them.

Rolland pulled on one of Whimsy's legs. "I'm stuck."

"Whoops, you forgot you can't climb up-side-down, didn't you?" Whimsy asked, smiling down at the roly stuck in the webs.

"I may have," Rolland said sheepishly. "I just had to find out what was below that trapdoor. I wanted to be the one to find something first."

"You silly roly," Whimsy said as she got the last of Rolland's legs free and put him on her back to hold onto.

Whimsy walked to the web shelves and pulled

the first box down. The lid came away with ease and they all got to see what the Wishweaver had been saving.

Inside the box was paper.

"It's just paper clippings." Whimsy couldn't help but be disappointed.

"Not just any paper clippings," Flit said. "Look at the heading!"

"Unanswered Wishes," Whimsy read.

"Whimsy, look at the date!" Rolland noticed.

She did. The date, along with the paper itself, was two years old. It was close to the time Whimsy had become a Sower of Seeds, and certainly after the Wishweaver had long since passed away.

"How long has someone been staying in this place?" Whimsy wondered.

She opened more boxes. They spanned the time since Whimsy had been around. She dug deeper.

She skipped down to a box at the very bottom, being careful not to upend the rest. This box was beginning to deteriorate with age. Whimsy felt butterflies flitting about in her stomach.

"How old is this one?" she wondered aloud.

"Open it up. That's what we're here for, isn't it? We all want to know more," Rolland said.

J.H. Winter

She opened the lid of the
oldest of the boxes
in the room.

The date was as far back as when the Wishweaver had vanished.

She sat back, her head spinning. "What does all this mean?"

"It means," came an unfamiliar voice from beneath them, "that I never left."

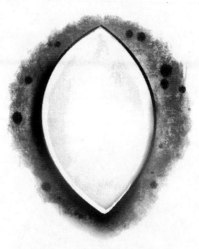

CHAPTER TWENTY-FOUR

MAGIC

Whimsy looked below the web she sat on and saw the reflection of several eyes staring back at her. Her heart raced as she scrambled to her feet.

The glistening eyes were gone. Whimsy looked back down into the dark hollow below just as the web floor began to rip.

The ripping continued, letting broken silk

hang useless to either side.

When the hole was cut wide enough, the one who had spoken to them stepped through.

******

"Miss… Miss Wishweaver?" Whimsy could barely get the words out.

"Call me Whisper, Whimsy."

"You know my name?" Whimsy couldn't believe it.

"I know a lot more than you can imagine."

"Do you know my name?" Flit asked.

Whisper laughed. "Indeed, Flit, and you must be Rolland. It's ever so nice to meet you both."

"I don't understand. We've never met you before. How do you know us at all?" Whimsy asked.

"Come inside and I'll do more than tell you," Whisper said, leading them back into her quaint home.

Whisper put a pot of water to boil on the embers that Whimsy had seen through the window. She added another log to the fire and it roared back to life.

Whimsy sat with her friends on Whisper's couch and Whisper took up the rocking chair by

the fireside. "This old body needs to stay warm," she said, throwing a patchwork blanket over herself.

"How old are you?" Whimsy asked.

"Don't you know it's not polite to ask your elders their age? Let's just say we Wishweavers don't age the same as other spiders do. From what I know, it all has to do with the magic we hold inside us. It keeps us going. At least for a time."

Whisper touched the spot between her two upper eyes where the same

familiar shape Whimsy had come to recognize in her own webs lay.

The pointed oval.

Whimsy had thought at first that Whisper had another eye in the center of her forehead that wasn't the same size, color, or shape as the others. Whimsy couldn't help but touch her own forehead as she watched the old Wishweaver. Whisper's forehead glowed at the very same moment. "I knew I was right," she said.

"Right about what?" Whimsy asked.

"Before I tell you that, I need you to know the rest of my story. I need you to know about the power of wishes."

CHAPTER TWENTY-FIVE
WISHES

"Let me start by saying being a Wishweaver has been the best thing that has ever happened to me. Being able to use my magic to help others get their wishes granted, to make them happy. That was always its own reward," Whisper began.

The kettle began to whistle on the fire and Whisper proceeded to pour the tea.

"Just water for me, thanks," Flit said. Seeds

didn't need anything but that.

"Right you are," Whisper said. "I haven't had a wisp in my midst in quite some time. I've missed them so. You all have such wonderful personalities. Certainly helped pass the time, hearing their stories of traveling on the West Wind and seeing Weyburn from above."

"You mean you talked with the wisps?" Whimsy asked. She'd thought she was the only one who did.

"Of course! How can you not? They make great company."

Whimsy squeezed Flit tighter and he smiled back at her.

With tea served hot, they each took a sip.

"I wish I had one of Lady Porcupine's crawler biscuits," Whisper said.

And there it was again. A wish that Whimsy could grant, and the reason she'd saved them in the first place.

Whimsy pulled out the last two biscuits and

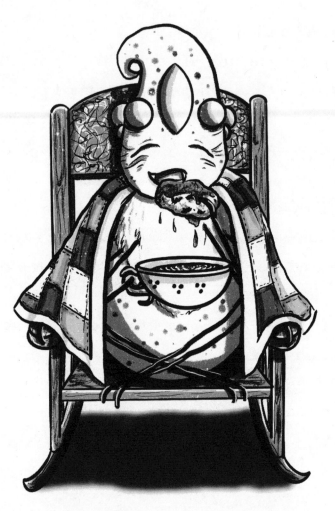

handed them to Whisper.

"I hoped she might have sent some along with you. I was just telling her recently that I'd run out," Whisper said, taking a bite of biscuit dipped in lavender tea.

"What do you mean, you were telling Lady Porcupine?" Whimsy asked through the steam of her own cup. "I thought no one in Weyburn knew you were still... well, that you were still alive."

"They don't. I'm getting ahead of myself here. Most of them don't know anyway. I've only kept in contact with a few of my dearest friends in Weyburn."

"Why's that?" Rolland asked.

"Because I blamed myself. For years, I blamed myself for what happened to Lenny the firefly and Mayflower Buffalo. Taking Lady's love so far away from her." Whisper shook her head in sadness.

"But none of that was your fault," Whimsy said. "Even May admits it was her fault for making such a ridiculous wish!"

"Perhaps. That's the thing about being a Wishweaver. It can be the best thing in the world. It can also be the worst.

"You see, I don't have control over the wishing.

That's
up to those
making wishes.
All I ever did was
catch the wisps, transfer
a sliver of my magic into
them for safekeeping, and wrap
them in webs to keep them together. This
way, the wisps couldn't float away, and they could
easily hold my magic until a wish-seeker broke
open the web, whispered what they wanted, and
set the magic free. The wisp got to take another

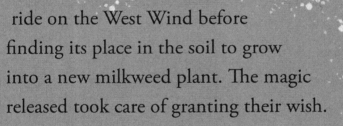

ride on the West Wind before
finding its place in the soil to grow
into a new milkweed plant. The magic
released took care of granting their wish.

Everyone was happy. Or, at least, that's
what I thought.

"Without having control over what the
wishers were asking for, my magic began to
be used for bad things. Not just bad,

but frivolous things. Things the wishers hadn't thought of the consequences of."

"Like Cricket asking to have hair?" Whimsy asked.

"Precisely. Cricket has no way of cutting hair. She's a crocodile, after all! Her legs don't work that way. They aren't intended to.

"So, what may have started off as an innocent request turned into a nuisance for her. A dangerous one, at that. So far, she's been okay, but what happens if her hair tangles her beneath the water's surface and she can't make it up to breathe? Cricket never thought of such consequences when she broke open my webs."

"I helped her tie her hair back, though. She'll be okay, at least for a little while," Whimsy said, knowing that Cricket's hair would continue to grow beyond the help of her ties.

"And I thank you for that. I can worry a little bit less now because you've been out there to help the others. Peter mentioned he'd met you in

Bellflower Grove."

"So, you talk to the fireflies, too?" Flit asked.

"They keep me in the know of what goes on in Weyburn. I couldn't let them think I'd left after what happened with poor Lennie. His death marked the end of my wishweaving. It was the last straw for me. When my wishes had finally ended the life of one of my friends, I knew I was done.

"Mayflower Buffalo being taken by the West Wind to the bottom of the waterfall was bad enough. I had torn two of my dearest friends apart, without any way of stopping it. The West Wind has always been like a brother to me. A brother who could go higher and farther than I ever could to help the wishes be granted. His own sort of magic, if you will. He has always worked with every Wishweaver since before my time."

Whimsy thought of Edmund and his fearlessness when it came to high places and swinging in the wind to build his webs. It made her smile to think of what they could do together now that she was no longer afraid.

"When Lennie's blue light stopped glowing in the belly of the frog that had eaten him, I felt my will to wishweave leave me. I'd grown weaker as my time of wishweaving drew to its natural close.

"I'd done enough to tear Weyburn apart even though I'd never meant for that to happen," Whisper finished.

"But it didn't tear them apart," Whimsy said. "If anything, you've brought them together again. Did you know that all of the animals in Weyburn help plant seedling wisps so that new milkweed pods can grow?

"We orb spiders work together to build webs half as good as the ones you were known to build, so that we can catch as many wisps as we can for the cycle to continue.

"I came here to have all of the questions inside my head answered. I had to know what we were all working together for. If there was no Wishweaver, it seemed like going through the motions of planting and capturing wisps wasn't the best way to spend our time. Now I know why I'm here."

"You do?" Whisper asked with a curious smile.

"I'm here to tell you to start again. I'm sure

that the wishes won't be what they were before. I'm sure the others in Weyburn have learned from their mistakes. They know now what happens when the Wishweaver is gone. Why do you think they have the 'Unanswered Wishes' column in the newspaper? I know you've been following them."

"I have, Whimsy," Whisper said. "And you're right. They have been wanting more generous things, just like they used to. The ridiculous wishing seems to have stopped. You're wrong about one thing, though."

"What's that?" Whimsy asked. Flit and Rolland leaned in to hear Whisper's answer. "That's not why you're here."

CHAPTER TWENTY-SIX
THE POINTED OVAL

"Then, why am I here?"

"When I made the decision to stop wishweaving, I knew that if I wanted there to be a chance of there being a future Wishweaver in Weyburn, I needed to save the last shred of magic I had for its final purpose. There was only one thing I had left to do. If I continued wishweaving at the time, I wouldn't have had the magic enough to do it.

"That meant that I couldn't give away any more wishes. I couldn't help undo the ones the wishers had made that had torn those in Weyburn apart. I had to let most of them think that I'd passed on. How else would I explain why I couldn't fix the way things had become? How else could I make sense of it all for them? That they could no longer have any more wishes."

"So, you had to wait for your magic to recharge so that you could be a Wishweaver again?" Whimsy was trying so hard to understand. She needed to.

"Not for me. My magic will never recharge. It's all but used up. I was told by the Wishweaver before me that, when I felt my magic was coming to its end—and she assured me I would know when that time was—I was to save it until the next Wishweaver came to take my place."

"The next Wishweaver?" Whimsy looked to Rolland and to Flit, who were already looking up at her in awe.

"Whim... Whim... Whimsy," Rolland stuttered, pointing at her.

She looked at Flit, who was silent for once in his life, looking from Whisper to Whimsy and back again.

"What is it?" Whimsy asked.

"They see it now," Whisper said.

"See what?"

Whisper walked over to Whimsy. The pointed oval on Whisper's forehead began to glow a vibrant myriad of colors. Whimsy couldn't tear her eyes away from the Wishweaver before her. Whisper brought a leg to her glowing forehead, then another to the same spot on Whimsy's.

The tingling feeling Whimsy had come to think of as a friendly figment of her imagination returned. It returned with a vengeance.

Colors burst around her. Blinded her.

She felt as though she was pulling them in. She had no idea how, but there was an energy, a magic, welling up inside of her. Filling her up.

Reaching into
dormant places
inside of her and
awakening them.
Memories of
wishes. Of magic.
Of happiness.
And even those
of pain. They all
found her.

What's happening? Whimsy yelled the question in her mind, but couldn't find the words to say them out loud. *Whisper!*

As the blinding light subsided and the magic inside her quieted, Whimsy opened her eyes. She looked around and saw that Whisper was gone.

"Where did Whisper go?" Whimsy asked, looking from Rolland to Flit, who had still not

managed to close their mouths after what they'd just witnessed with their own eyes.

"Where's the Wishweaver?" Whimsy asked, panicked now. She hadn't seen what had happened to Whisper. Her heart sank. Tears welled inside her. "Rolland?"

He was still in shock.

She looked at Flit. He always had the answers. Flit reached up for her.

She brought him up to rest his forehead to hers as he'd done so many times before. This was his answer.

With a flash of lavender light illuminating the room, Whimsy felt magic awaken again inside of her. She knew what she would find if she reached up to her forehead.

"It's okay, Whimsy," Flit said, knowing his part to play.

"I don't understand," she said, renewed tears pouring out of her.

"Yes, you do. I'm ready now."

Whimsy heard an ancient language fill her mind, and her mouth moved to allow the words to be free. With them came a sliver of magic.

Wishweaver magic.

Magic enough to grant a single wish.

******

"This feels amazing!" Flit said, now glowing a lavender color himself because of Whimsy's magic.

"What does it feel like?" Whimsy asked.

"Can you give me some magic, too?" Rolland asked.

"I don't think so," Whimsy said. "I'm pretty sure the magic wouldn't stick. From the stories that were once told about the Wishweaver, the prior ones had tried lots of different things to hold their magic before finding that the wisps were the best at keeping it until the wishes were made."

"Ha! See. There is something I'm good at!" Flit said. "I may not be able to move on my own, but I know I can do this! I was born to!"

Rolland rolled his eyes.

"Anyway, I'm supposed to wrap you in webs now… I think." Whimsy said. "I wish Whisper was here. I feel like I still have so many questions."

"You're always going to have questions," Flit said. "That's good, though. It's good to question things. Come up with new, better ways of doing them. That's why I know you're going to be an amazing Wishweaver, Whimsy! You'll figure out a way to make your magic count. Now, wrap me up already!"

Whimsy laughed, but started to spin her webs.

She spun them until there was no chance Flit was going anywhere on his own. "Okay in there?" she asked.

"Sleepy now. I think I'll take a little nap."

Whimsy smiled as she heard the familiar sounds of Flit snoring.

Whimsy looked to Rolland. "Shall we?" she asked.

"Shall we what?" Rolland asked.

"I've a few old wishes to set right," Whimsy said.

"And after that?" he asked as they walked out the front door of the Wishweaver house.

She brought out the key that had worked to open the trapdoor in the floor. She tried the lock again and found that, this time around, it fit perfectly.

"After that, I spin my webs. My darling wisps will be here soon, and with them, a new season for wishing."

The End.

Until next wishing season…

ABOUT THE AUTHOR

J.H. Winter loves to create. She writes for children and teens. She draws. She crochets amigurumi. She even hops behind the camera and teaches how to crochet on YouTube!

When she isn't holding a pen or crochet hook, she hosts crochet-alongs and shares what she's working on creatively, over on her blog (http://blog.jhwinter.com) and YouTube channel (http://www.youtube.com/inkstitches), Ink & Stitches.

J.H. Winter's published works include the illustration of the *Theodore and the Enchanted Bookstore* series, published by Incorgnito Publishing Press. Starting with book four, *Fairy Flights and Neverland Nights* (Aug. 2020), she will fill the shoes of both author and illustrator of the series. Now, she not only gets to continue drawing that curious corgi, Theodore, she also gets to decide which stories he'll jump into next!

She wrote the illustrated chapter book, *Tales of Whimsy: Wishweaver* (set for a Sept. 2020 release), originally as a picture book, but it had much too much magic to contain in a mere 32 pages. So, Whimsy got her way—as she often does—and got to journey into a much bigger adventure. A series of adventures to be exact. Her wisp friend and co-adventurer, Flit, approved of this decision.

As life would have it, J.H. Winter shares her writerly and creative life with her two precocious kids, her equally-imaginative husband, and their frisky feline, Merlin. Verdict is still out as to whether he is in fact a wizard.

Find out more on social media @jhwinterauthor, or visit her website at www.jhwinter.com.

ACKNOWLEDGEMENTS

Writing and illustrating *Wishweaver* has been the best, most difficult, and easily most rewarding creative project I've ever taken on. I couldn't have made this tale a reality without the help of my husband, and most avid supporter, Sean. He told me to write my story down, and I've written down every one since. He pushed me toward learning digital illustration, and his encouragement allowed me to take on an entirely new medium for my art and I'm ever so glad he did. Thanks for keeping me sane and grounded always.

For my two sweets, James and Lizzie. Their brilliant personalities soar through the pages of my stories in the characters that journey through them. Thank you both for the endless material and hugs.

I can never say enough thanks to my inspiring parents, Bert and Bonnie, for their unwavering love and support, and for teaching me the beauty in bugs and books.

Without my brother, Aaron, I'd have no one to compare my hard work to. He has always pushed me to push myself and has shared in every success. Also, to his wife, and my dear friend, Jenny. She has always believed in me, even when my doubts ran high, and when I need an artistic opinion, I always know who to turn to!

Thanks to my in-laws, Diane, Paul, and Kristen. They taught me never to settle, that I have to strive for more, and to believe in my own abilities. I hope this book proves that I've done just that.

When I first wrote *Wishweaver*, it began as a picture book, written during a class I was taking taught by author/illustrator, Arree Chung, in Storyteller Academy. With Arree's guidance and knowledge, Whimsy's tale went through countless revisions. Arree told me, I had done a wonderful job of painting the world and the characters, but I needed to focus on just one story. It was a picture book after all, at the time. I realized then, thanks to Arree, that this story had so much more than could fit in 500 words or less. Turning this into a chapter book series and allowing Whimsy to truly tell her tale, was exactly what she needed.

Storyteller Academy also led me to my dedicated critique group, the Story Stitchers: Amy, Laura, Kristy N, and Amanda.

Thanks for putting up with countless revisions, where we worked together to make sure that the wishing process made sense. You never gave up on Whimsy, and pushed me to keep on until I could get her story just right.

I want to say a big thanks to Alison Williams, the first editor to hold *Wishweaver*, for being the first to realize that I'd done what I set out to do with Whimsy's tale and had finally gotten it just right. Her encouragement that I'd made a beautiful story, is what kept me pushing forward to find Whimsy a home.

Unending thanks to Incorgnito Publishing Press, and to Michael Conant, for truly seeing the vision I had for this story and taking a chance on a project of an entirely different magnitude than he'd ever worked on before. He allowed me to break the mold, to make my vision for *Wishweaver* a reality, and I am eternally grateful.

Thanks also to Daria Lacy, who went through countless proofs to get over 120 illustrations on their proper pages and all that goes along with formatting said artwork, so that the illustrations and text work together to create a beautiful book to hold in your hands.

Thanks must be said for my final editor, Jennifer Collins, as well as my cover designer, Star Foos. Jennifer loved this book from the beginning, helping me know I'd succeeded in telling Whimsy's tale. Star was a trooper when it came to adjustments on the cover design and I greatly appreciate all the back and forth she put up with to get it just right.

A special thank you goes out to all of my fellow writing and library friends, for always asking how my stories were coming along. Thanks for taking such an active interest in my work, and reading the early drafts, giving such positive feedback and support. Their interest in what I do, propels me forward every day: Rebecca, Jackie, Renee, Kristy C, Yu-Chieh, Amytha, Shoshana, Cindy, K. Kibbee, and Allison M.

And finally, to a neighbor years back who noticed and made mention of a "spiderweb catching wishes." She never knew the idea those three words had sparked inside me, and just like a wisp, away we flew!

~ Julianne

CROCHET YOUR VERY OWN WHIMSY AND FLIT!

Not only is J.H. Winter, an author and illustrator, she's also a whiz with a crochet hook!

Her whimsical designs are shared on her blog and YouTube channel: Ink & Stitches!

To get your free pattern to create your very own Whimsy, along with her best friend, Flit, head over to her blog.

http://blog.jhwinter.com

Don't know how to crochet? Not to worry! She's got you covered there too, on Ink & Stitches YouTube!

https://www.youtube.com/inkstitches

CREDITS

This book is a work of art produced by
Incorgnito Publishing Press; Corgi Bits Imprint

Jennifer Collins
Editor

J. H. Winter
Author and Illustrator

Star Foos
Designer

Janice Bini
Chief Reader

Michael Conant
Publisher

Daria Lacy
Graphic Production

September 2020
Incorgnito Publishing Press